Keeping Up With The Jones

SOLA PRODUCTIONS, INC.
PHILADELPHIA

Keeping Up With The Jones

Solomon Jones

 Published in the United States by Sola Productions, Inc.

Jones, Solomon

Keeping Up With The Jones/ Solomon Jones.

ISBN 0-9755219-0-X

Excerpts from the following songs are included in the story "Sesame Seeds" :

Conjunction Junction
Music and Lyrics Bob Dorough

I'm Just A Bill
Music and Lyrics Dave Frishberg

Preamble
Music and Lyrics Lynn Ahrens

Printed in the United States of America

Illustrations by James McHugh

Book design by Solomon Jones

For my brilliant wife, LaVeta, whose ideas made these stories possible. And for my daughter, Eve, who is funny without trying to be.

Acknowledgments

First, I must thank my Lord and Savior Jesus Christ, without whom none of this would be possible. My deepest gratitude to my beautiful wife, LaVeta, who I often approach with the words: "Okay, so what am I writing about *this* week?" Thankfully, she always has the answer. Thanks to my daughter, Eve, whose antics fueled much of what is contained in these pages. I am forever grateful to my mother, Carolyn, my aunt Juanita, and my grandmother, Lula, all of whom taught me to laugh in the face of adversity. And to my daughter, Adrianne. I love you. Thanks to the *Philadelphia Weekly* for publishing these stories as columns, and for helping me every step of the way as I worked to bring this project to fruition. Thanks to Tim Whitaker. And a special thanks to Sara Kelly, who wrote the headlines to each of these stories. Thanks to Jeff Cox, who lays out the column weekly, and to Jim McHugh, whose vibrant illustrations bring life to each one of these anecdotes. And of course, thanks to you, my readers. You are the mirror that reflects the essence of each story I tell. Get ready to laugh . . . It's going to be a fun ride.

Also by Solomon Jones

Ride Or Die
The Bridge
Pipe Dream

Keeping Up With The Jones

Marriage

Sole Survivor

LaVeta bought bobos. It was the shock of my married life.

Where I come from, there are a few things you just don't do. You don't disrespect your mother. You don't try to hustle a hustler. And never, under any circumstances, do you wear bobos.

What are bobos?

Simply put, bobos are extremely cheap sneakers. Dollar ninety-nine cheap. Back in the day, they were the kind of sneakers you could buy from a wire mesh container next to the checkout counter at Pantry Pride. You know, white canvas, hard yellow rubber, dried brown glue oozing from the sides.

Bobos.

When I was growing up, if your mom bought you bobos instead of Jack Purcells or Pro-Keds, you prayed they weren't the kind with the conspicuous red or blue stripe running around the side. If they were (and God was especially merciful), your mom scraped up another $1.99 before the rubber began to crack.

When you got your new bobos, you threw the old ones up on the wire at the end of the block. Then you tried your best to wear out the new ones quickly, hoping your mom would get the message and buy you something better next time.

Long and short of it, bobos are bad news, and everyone from my generation knows it.

So when I came home last week and my wife, LaVeta, said, "Honey, I got some new sneakers," I was expecting something along the lines of Nike Airs.

But when she removed them from the box, they were something else altogether. White leather with red stripes, rubber that was white instead of yellow, an intricate logo on the top. There was no denying it. Neither the quality of the material nor the fancy logo could hide the horrible truth.

Bobos.

"They're not bobos!" LaVeta said defensively. Oh, but they were. They were manufactured by some company called the Beverly Hills Polo Club. I don't know what that means in Beverly Hills. But in Philadelphia, it means they're bobos.

I looked down at the sneakers and smiled. Then I reached over and picked up our 1-year-old daughter, Eve.

"Mommy's got bobos," I said sadly.

Eve said, "Da da."

Then she looked down at the sneakers, glanced at me and smiled at her mother. She didn't get it. At least not yet.

"I was trying to save us some money," my wife said earnestly.

That's when I knew my wife loved me.

You would have to love someone to wear bobos for the greater good. Granted, I'm the sole bread-winner--we decided that my wife would stay at home and take care of our daughter--but I would never have asked her to do anything that drastic for the sake of our financial life.

You would have to love someone to wear bobos for the greater good.

And to tell you the truth, I couldn't understand why a summa cum laude college graduate, a woman who likes the finer things in life, a woman who I thought understood the cultural nuances of being black and in your mid-30s, would buy a pair of bobos.

Even to keep our cash flow healthy. Even out of love for her husband.

As she started to explain that they were not, in fact, bobos, I began to imagine the various whispered insults we'd have to endure.

"Sol," her cousin Dana would say. "What's with LaVeta's sneakers? You need a couple dollars?"

The people at our church would take up a collection. My mother would pretend not to notice. The neighbors would sit on their steps speaking in hushed tones.

But the worst thing of all would be the song. Yes, the history of bobos is so storied that there's a song about them. It goes something like this:

Bobos, they make your feet feel fiiiiiine.
Bobos, they cost a dollar ninety-niiiiiine.
Bobos
Come get your bobos
Come get your bobos, your bobos, todaaay.

I couldn't let LaVeta keep them. So with the bobos refrain still reverberating in my head, I began to plot the bobos' disappearance. I would throw them in the trash. I would burn them in a bonfire.

But then, just as my evil scheme was beginning to take shape, she dropped the bombshell.

"As a matter of fact," LaVeta said triumphantly, "I bought two pairs."

I looked down at the cloth sneakers she pulled from another box, and as my face crumpled in disbelief, the truth, in all its ugliness, burst from my lips.

"You bought two pairs of bobos?" I asked incredulously.

She laughed.

Then our daughter, with all the wisdom she'd gained over the first year of her life, looked at me, pointed down at the sneakers and, in the sheepish voice of a child pronouncing a new phrase for the first time, she said it.

"Buh buh?"

"That's right," I said with resignation. "Bobos."

Eve hasn't stopped looking down at those sneakers and saying "bobos" since.

Frankly, neither have I.

Blowing Smoke

Pot addiction can rip apart the best of families

My wife, LaVeta, is a pothead. You can't look at her and see evidence of her addiction. She's still as beautiful as she was on our first date. But looks can be deceiving. Fact of the matter is, LaVeta's pot addiction is tearing our family apart.

All the telltale signs are there. She's spending too much money and is up at night tracking her pot purchases. She talks about pot constantly. She's copped as much as 17 pounds at one time.

She's got connections sending her different kinds of pot from all over the country--from Nevada Red to California Silver, Black and Blue.

The pot dealers are so ruthless, so brazen, that they send catalogs and emails right to our home. Worse, they dangle little pot-filled gold boxes whenever LaVeta logs onto our computer.

It's been painful to watch this pot addiction drag her down. I've asked our family, our friends--and now I'm calling on you, my readers, to intervene. We're gonna beat this thing. And we're gonna start by outing the pot dealers--right now, right here.

All you people at Cooking.com, Amazon.com and Epicurious.com, I'm putting you on notice. You barked up the wrong tree when you got Solomon Jones' wife on pot!

When I first confronted LaVeta, she smiled defiantly and told me how her addiction began.

"It started innocently. You start off as a foodie," she said. "And then it goes from food to cookware. You can't have one without the other. I began by going to Epicurious.com, looking up recipes. Cooking.com is an advertiser on the Epicurious site. They must have advertised some kind of special. The first pot I ordered was cast iron--$49.95.

"And then I went back."

Once, twice, and before we knew it, these pot sites had become an obsession. LaVeta's ordered so much pot we can't fit it all into our kitchen.

Last August she ordered a Calphalon anodized aluminum flat bottom wok (which is not technically a pot, if you ask potheads, though it sits on the stove and cooks stuff just like any other pot).

"I got it for $79.99!" she told me when I began tallying the pot purchases.

I wasn't convinced. I think 80 bucks is a lot for a wok. After all, we already had a perfectly good wok that we'd bought from the Chinese market on Race Street for $15.

Sadly, after I spoke up, the rationalization--one of the hallmarks of pot addiction--began in earnest.

"Calphalon products, if you go to Williams-Sonoma or some other store, will cost about $130," she said. "But this was on sale, and I'd been wanting a wok. I got that and some glass mixing bowls, and they were on sale for $11.99. I think they were originally $22 or $23."

Look, all I'm saying, whether it be a wok or a pot or any other kind of household utensil: Do it in moderation.

But as I watch what is happening here, I know that moderation is not an option.

After she bought the cast iron pot and the wok, LaVeta bought an 8-quart, heavy-gauge steel, enamel-coated stock pot for $59.99 and several other pots I don't know anything about.

Soon she was spending hours at a time online, particularly at Amazon.com.

Amazon kept track of her pot purchases, from

the $179.99 Le Creuset 7-quart Dutch oven coated with enamel (which comes with a free precision-pour saucepan--a $49.99 value!) to the cookbooks she purchased for $20.97 apiece.

They profiled her and put together a daily list of stuff, then dangled the items in a sparkling gold box in the corner of her personal Amazon webpage.

She began reading reviews from other pot fanatics. People like Tom, of Oconomowoc, Wisc., who says his Lodge 7-quart Dutch oven "absorbs, distributes and retains heat beautifully, as advertised."

Such reviews, according to LaVeta, are the gospel.

"Great minds think alike," she says. "Obviously they're potheads, too."

But the reviews aren't the worst of it. The pot dealers offer an online tracking system that allows buyers to track the progress of their purchases as they make their way across the country.

Sometimes I'm awakened in the middle of the night by the sound of our computer and LaVeta's little fingers, pointing and clicking as she tracks her latest pot purchase.

I've asked her to get help. But she's refused to do anything about her pot fixation.

"I'm not ready to take step one," she says. "I know I have a problem, but I don't want help just yet. It's my decision to make."

An intervention hasn't yet been planned.

Where's the feminine products aisle?

If you're man enough to ask that question at the drug store, you're man enough to get married.

Single Guy, if you're considering marriage, consider this: In the new millennium it's as important for a husband to know his way around a drug store as it is for him to know his way around a leaky faucet.

Why? Because there will be times when your wife will be in need of, um, essentials. You know, the once-a-month essentials. The kind of essentials men don't need.

It's times like these that separate the men from the boys. If you really love her, feminine hygiene shouldn't even be an issue.

Because when your wife is trapped inside with the monthly visitor knocking at the door and you get that cell phone call, you've got to step up.

Sure, Single Guy, you're reading this, and you're saying, "Come on! It can't be that hard! You walk in, get the goods and leave."

Well, son, there's more to it than that. That's why married guys call it the Mission.

I don't care if you've fought wars, wrestled crocodiles or run triathlons. If you ain't navigated the feminine hygiene aisle at the drug store, you ain't done jack. Me? I've completed the Mission. And this is my story.

It was a rainy day. My wife, who was incapacitated at the time, sent me to the drug store to get the goods.

I couldn't protest. She couldn't do it for herself. So I steeled myself for the journey. And then--dressed as a hoodlum in black skull cap, leather jacket, Timberland boots and black jeans--I walked inside.

Quickly, I zigzagged through the store, searching those little overhead signs for the words "feminine hygiene." When I couldn't find the correct aisle, I became angry.

Scowling, I approached a drug store employee and posed the question with all the bravado required of a man trapped in my situation.

"Where is the feminine products aisle?" I asked, deepening my voice.

The worker's jaw dropped. She looked me up and down. She was obviously new and hadn't yet borne witness to a husband on the Mission. Unable to speak, she just pointed.

"Thanks," I said, trying to sound nonchalant.
As I turned, I felt her eyes. They were following me.

When I entered the feminine hygiene aisle, I was confronted with shelf upon shelf of womanly stuff. There were tampons, sprays, powders, pads and wipes--and all in countless brands, sizes, shapes and colors.

By the time I spotted the Always brand my wife had requested, there were matronly looking, blue-haired women walking by, trying not to stare.

"Must find the goods," I thought, staring at the shelves with single-minded determination.

As I searched the shelves, I learned that some marketing genius at Procter and Gamble (the company that makes Always) had decided they would make 50 different products. Among them: Slender with Flexi-Wings. Regular. Regular with Flexi-Wings. Super Long. Super Long with Flexi-Wings. Overnight with Flexi-Wings. And that was just the Ultras. Let's not get into the Maxis.

To make matters worse, they were color-coded. Some had yellow stripes. Some had orange stripes. Some had green stripes.

My head was reeling. More matronly women walked by. I whipped out my cell phone and called my wife.

"Is it Ultra Thin, Maxis, Overnight, Flexi-Wings or what?" I asked in a panicky stage whisper.

When we settled on the type, I grabbed the color-coded package and half ran, trying in vain to escape the prying eyes of the women who were either amused or alarmed--it's a fine line--by the sight of a man in the feminine hygiene aisle.

Now there was only one remaining hurdle. The counter.

As I approached the two teenage girls working the registers, I flashed my wedding ring in an effort to prove that I wasn't some weirdo who was just into feminine products.

Thankfully, they were caught up in compulsive teenage girl conversation.

"She stupid," one said derisively. "She lettin' him use her."

"Ummmm hmmm."

I slid the package onto the counter, once again flashing the wedding ring.

"Cash or charge?" the girl asked, disinterested.

"Debit card."

"Punch in your code."

I did as I was asked, grabbed the bag and flew out the door.

Mission complete.

So why do I tell you this? I tell you, Single Guy, because someone has to warn you now about the truth.

If you wanna get married in the new millennium, you've got to be man enough to go to your neighborhood drug store and walk the feminine hygiene aisle. Because I don't care how much you say you love her. If you don't know the difference between a Super Thin Ultra Long with Flexi-Wings and an Overnight Maxi with Wings, you're just not ready to be a husband.

Period.

The Target of My Desire

Confessions of a date starved husband.

Eight years ago, when I was a single guy starring in my own version of The Bachelor--let's call it Single 'n the Hood--this was my ritual. Three times a week I would take a long bath, spray on some Joop! cologne, throw on my new clothes and go out on the town.

That's when I was mackin' the honeys. Picking from a select few whom I would accompany to fancy restaurants and movie theaters as part of my show.

But on July 5, 1997, after my first date with LaVeta, I voted everybody else off. LaVeta won. That is if winning is having a loud, active 18-month-old, bills up the yin yang, a husband with three jobs and all the other blessings and problems that come with married life.

I won, too, I guess. At this very moment my Joop! bottle is empty, and we forgot to buy deodorant last week, so I'm picking the white stuff out of the corners of my Sure stick and smearing it under my arms. Fancy restaurants? Most have my picture in the window, accompanied by the words: "Have you seen this man?"

Things have gotten so bad that last Friday, when my wife asked me if I wanted to go to Target to buy baby clothes for Eve, not only did I agree, but I eagerly said yes when she suggested we top off our evening with a trip to the Old Town Buffet.

That was when I knew I'd hit rock bottom.

When we walked into Target, Eve was in the shopping cart seat doing her usual bit, waving at her adoring fans. LaVeta was doing her Target thing, too. Mouth twitching at the corners. Eyes dancing from one sale sign to another. Skin bathed in the glow of the overhead fluorescent lighting as her shopping addiction seeped out like sweat.

That look usually means that our Target trip will last for hours, leaving me curled up in the fetal position on the polished floor in the housewares aisle, muttering the words, "Help meeeee. Somebody help meeee."

But this trip was different. I was there, in Target, and I was smiling, cracking jokes, pointing out the many pregnant women with kids tugging at their skirts.

Oh, Lord. It was almost like I was ... glad to be there.

I didn't think it could get worse. But when we went up to the toddler clothing section, it did.

I didn't think it could get worse. But when we went up to the toddler clothing section, it did.

I parked the cart next to the toddler summer wear, and Eve began to play with the clothes on the rack while I pretended I could contribute to the discussion.

"How about this one?" I asked, pulling out a pastel-colored cotton size 3T shirt while LaVeta browsed the coordinates.

Her eyes said, "The toddler aisle in Target is my turf. And don't you forget it!"

Her mouth, though, said something totally different.

"That's nice, honey. But I don't think they have anything to match that top."

A few more exchanges like that and I got the point. I stayed in a man's place. Credit card at the ready, mouth shut, pushing the cart, playing with the kid.

That's when the other mothers and grandmothers invaded the aisle.

"Mikey, get over here! I'm not going to buy you anything if you don't get over here right now!"

"Jamal, get offa that! That's why you don't get to go anywhere! You don't know how to act!"

The kids, of course, ignored all warnings, threats and shouting. They knew they were there to run wild, and like good little soldiers, they did their part.

My nerves were shot by the time we left for the restaurant.

Old Town Buffet? What's not to like? Nothing like all-you-can-eat food to cheer up a husband after he's been used to satisfy the shopping itch.

I loaded up on crab legs, fried chicken, mashed potatoes and corn. Stuff was actually pretty good. LaVeta--worldly woman that she is--had sushi and Mongolian beef.

Eve did her usual. She ate ours. Well, everything except the Mongolian beef. It was kind of tough. Should've been, I guess. It probably didn't get any closer to Mongolia than South Philly. And you know they make 'em tough in South Philly.

For our next date, we'll do our usual. Movies? A bad flick from Blockbuster. Dinner? Wendy's drive-thru. Anything that requires more than two hours alone? We'll call our mothers, of course. And tell them to take the kid to Target.

Junk Food Jones

If we keep eating like this, we'll weigh a ton in no time.

My family is caught in the throes of snack addiction. It's painful to admit, but I'm afraid that if I don't say something now, we'll all drown in milk chocolate, pretzels and nougat (whatever that is).

Don't believe me? As I was preparing to write this column, I was eating a bite-sized Snickers--one of the many delicacies that stock our gargantuan candy jar--and my daughter, Eve, walked up to me and grabbed my arm.

With the Herculean strength of a candy fiend trying to score a fix, she pulled my hand down to her mouth and took a bite.

I thought she would stop after that. But her candy jones was just too strong. She chewed that first tasty morsel while humming a Snickers-eatin' tune and dancin' a little jig. When she finished her production number, she was back, tugging at my arm until she'd forced another bite into her mouth.

I knew it wouldn't be long before she ate the whole thing. And so, in an effort to keep the peace, I offered her another bite. She turned her head and refused to take it.

Taking up Eve's Snickers-eatin' hum while dancing in my chair, I happily ate the rest. And that's when I knew.

All three of us--LaVeta, Eve, and myself--have junk food addictions. And we all have a junk food drug of choice.

Eve's is cake. And it's been that way since her first birthday. I saw it when, rather than fawning over the frosted Tweety that graced her birthday cake, she ruthlessly chewed away at the poor defenseless bird.

While everyone stood around laughing at the cuteness of this Tweety massacre, I saw a glint in her eye. The kind that junk food junkies get when the rush hits them just right.

It was then that I knew I should be afraid. Very afraid.

You see, Eve, like all children, has obsessive-compulsive tendencies. If she likes a particular game, she makes us play it over and over again. I've played peekaboo, for example, until my palms were raw and bloody. Okay, maybe I didn't actually start bleeding, but if blood would have made it stop, I would have.

That's why the cake incident frightened me. I mean, suppose she doesn't grow out of her obsessive-compulsive stage? Suppose she stays that way?

Suppose she turns into Eve, the cake fiend mom? Can you see it?

"Rufus, bring me another piece o' that chocolate cake, boy!"

"But Mom, I can't fit through your bedroom door. You're too big."

"Don't you sass me, boy! You bring that cake in here or I'm gonna whip you good."

"But Mom, you can't whip me. You can't even move. You weigh 1,000 pounds."

"Don't you get technical with me!"

Because such images have haunted me for

almost a year, I've considered doing something about our junk food habits. You know, trying to put forth a good example for Eve's sake.

Problem is, LaVeta and I are even worse than the kid.

LaVeta has been carrying on a decades-long relationship with Doritos. And though she denies it, she often hides ice cream in the back of the freezer, behind rock-hard hamburger, dead-eyed whiting and leftover collard greens.

Then there are the soft pretzels. In her obsessive-compulsive little junk food world, my wife will only eat the ones from the end.

But even with Eve's cake fixation and LaVeta's peculiar fascination with Doritos, ice cream and pretzels, I think my junk food dependency is the worst. You see, I've developed a junk food ritual.

My day begins with a trip to the candy jar, where I grab Now and Laters, Jaw Breakers and Tootsie Rolls. If Snickers are near the top of the jar, I stuff them quickly into my pockets with a fiendish sneer.

Sometimes I even do the candy dance.

When I arrive at work, I eat donuts--at least two--because Dunkin' Donuts has that special. Then at noon I eat hamburgers, hoagies, cheesesteaks or fried chicken. And despite my co-workers' relentless teasing, I must eat these items at my desk. It's part of my ritual.

Finally, there are the Baby Ruth binges. There's a guy who sells them for 55 cents--a full nickel cheaper than those shysters who sell them for 60. The way I see it, if I buy 12 at 55 cents apiece, I get the 13th free!

I know. It's sick. But I'm putting it out there because I--no, *we*--need help.

But until we take the first step and decide to enter family junk food therapy, I've got a question for you. Are you gonna finish that Snickers?

Marriage - a retrospective

Three's the charm.

Just celebrated my third wedding anniversary. Lots of stuff to reflect upon. But I gotta be careful. Because if I say too much, my wife--yes, little innocent LaVeta--will do what any good wife would do. She'll take one of her 50-pound Le Crueset pots, and she'll go upside my head.

Sure, I'm afraid of having a pot-shaped dent in my skull. But sometimes you've gotta take one for the team. And brothers (for the purposes of this exercise, non-blacks are hereby deputized as brothers), I am on your team.

That's right. It don't matter about me now. I've been to the mountaintop. I've been to the valley low. I've been to the other side. And gentlemen, I've lived to tell about it.

So read this column, and know that you may see me with a pot-shaped dent in my head next week.

But remember, men, I will have taken that dent for you.

Year One

If you're anything like we were, you will be impoverished. But you'll be in love. And as long as you don't try to go nowhere and buy nothin' with love, you'll be okay.

We were so poor, the bedroom in our studio apartment doubled as the family room, the hallway leading to the kitchen was my office, and the bathroom served as a den ... with a toilet.

Our place was so small that the varmints would tell me to move over when the Eagles game came on, then make me share my nachos. But hey, it was home.

That's why, in the pioneering spirit of the newly married, we affectionately named our little nest *Love Jones*. It was tight, but it was right. I mean, what husband wouldn't want a place where he never has to chase his wife more than 10 feet to get his just due? Of course, such convenience comes with a price.

Six months into the party, I was standing at the sink washing dishes when LaVeta dropped the bombshell.

"Did you enjoy yourself the other day?" she asked.

I said yeah.

"You willing to pay for it for the next 18 years?"

Party over.

Year Two

If you, like us, have thoroughly enjoyed year one, and your wife is now pregnant, you will learn to laugh at yourselves in year two.

Us? We took a trip to New Orleans to celebrate the start of our second year. In July. While LaVeta was with child. Have you ever been to New Orleans in July? Man-eating mosquitoes that travel in packs. Humidity hanging on your shoulders like a buffalo pelt. Drunken tourists heaving on Bourbon Street.

But all in all, Nawlins is a pretty nice place. Friendly people. Great jazz. French donuts. Po Boys. If you can just remember to watch your step on the vomit-soaked sidewalks, you'll enjoy it.

Now, where was I? Ah yes. Year two.

By October of that year, LaVeta was ready to have the baby. But Eve liked it in there. Her specialty was kicking, poking and prodding LaVeta's organs. Very interesting to watch. Looked like a scene out of *Alien*.

Anyhoo, little Eve was born and came to live with us in *Love Jones*. Except there wasn't a whole lotta love goin' on anymore. Not with little Eve screaming all night long.

And after we decided that my wife would stay home to take care of the baby, we were not only sleep-deprived. We were money-deprived, too.

At my lowest point, I considered moonlighting at Rite Aid.

Year Three

We moved last year. Relative said he was giving us a house. We put a pretty penny into fixing up the place, which was in such bad shape when we moved in that a contractor asked us, "Was this house abandoned?"

"Uh, no."

After we renovated, our charitable relative changed his mind (note to self: Never trust charitable relatives). We ended up moving again, and we're preparing to move once more. In fact, we've moved so much since we got hitched that whenever we pass a U-Haul place, the clerks smile, wave and thank me for putting their kids through college.

But despite the ups and downs, three years of marriage has made me love my wife even more than I did when we walked down the aisle. More than that, it's made me strong. And it's a good thing, too.

I'm gonna need all the strength I can muster when LaVeta reads this and goes upside my head with one of those 50-pound pots.

Fred Sanford Slept Here

My Philly house hunt has a laugh track.

Remember when I said we've moved so many times that U-Haul clerks often thank me for paying their kids' college tuition?

Well, some of those clerks might have to think about sending their snot-nosed brats to community college. Because by the time you read this, our search for a home may be over.

I've worked hard to get to this point--even toiled to erase youthful indiscretions from my credit report. And cleaning up credit is no small task. Because credit, in case you didn't know, is the permanent record your teacher told you about when you were a kid.

"Solomon, if you shoot one more spit ball ... "

Whoosh. Splat!

"That's it. I'm calling Experian, TransUnion and Equifax. This is going on your permanent record!"

That's right. I had everything on my credit report from student loans and electric bills to an unfortunate nose-picking incident that was caught on an ATM video camera back in the '90s.

Around March of 2003, through a stream of letters, documents and payments, I managed to get most of it cleaned up. And when I did, I had something that most people don't have. I had hope.

And so, with my newfound creditworthiness to boost me, I set about the task of trying to find my family a home.

This is my story.

The mortgage companies always tell you that you can afford a huge mortgage, because the more money you borrow, the more money they make. If you can't pay it, they can always foreclose on the house.

Greed is the game, baby. And the realty companies play it, too.

"So, Mrs. Jones, this 18th-century colonial is a bargain at $1 million. Don't you think so, Mr. Jones?"

"I ... uh ... think so."

When we came to our senses and started looking at row houses, our experiences grew increasingly weird, beginning with a small twin "fixer-upper" in West Mount Airy.

It wasn't the rain forest quality of the overgrown backyard that frightened us. It wasn't even the doors-off-the-hinges interior with creaky floors and spiderweb-like cracks snaking up the painted walls.

It was the neighbors. They were old.

And when old men sit around on their porch smoking cheap cigars and drinking soda out of jelly jars, with old cars parked on the grass, it can mean only one thing. They're fugitives from the set of *Sanford and Son*.

As we toured the house, I kept imagining the theme song, complete with bluesy harmonica. And when we stepped outside and saw Fred, Grady, Bubba and the gang from the pool hall telling jokes and swapping lies, I kept waiting for Lamont to come bouncing down the street in an old truck.

"Um, I don't think we're gonna be bidding on that house," I later told our realtor.

Fortunately, she understood.

Later, we looked at a row house in West Oak Lane. The house was cheap, and I'd made LaVeta come and see it, despite her concerns about the neighborhood.

"It's not that bad," I'd told her. "We have to look at a place we can afford."

She just gave me that sister-girl look and said, "Ummm hmm."

Translation: "You're a fool, but I'm not gonna say

anything, because I want you to see for yourself that you're a fool."

Because she'd said "Ummm hmm," I had to do what men do. I had to pretend it didn't bother me when I saw a cop move some boys off the corner. I kept up the facade pretty well. Until I met the neighbors.

"Man, y'all like the fourth family to look at this house today," said a twenty-something man who sat on the steps with his friend. "Y'all better hurry up and cop this jawn."

"Do you live here?" I asked.

"Nah, I live next door."

This guy--let's call him Rollo--was apparently a man of leisure who had time to watch everyone come and go. I thought of him as we toured the well-kept house.

When we left, Rollo had one final question.

"Excuse me, sir. What do you do?"

"I work downtown," I said.

"Oh. You look like this guard I know."

From prison, no doubt.

"I don't think we're gonna cop that jawn," I later told our realtor.

"Ummm hmm," said LaVeta, looking at our realtor, who was a sister, too.

“Ummm hmm,” our realtor replied. Like any sister worth her salt, she understood.

Keep On Truckin'

Forget safe streets as long as I'm behind the wheel.

If you spotted a shiny black head bouncing behind the steering wheel of a 24-foot-long Ryder truck last Saturday, it was me, the guy least qualified to drive such a monstrosity.

That's right--Solomon Jones, driving through Philadelphia--first along the hilly, serpentine strip of Ridge Avenue that winds through Roxborough, then along the pothole-ridden bone-thin length of Washington Lane that runs from Germantown Avenue to Chelten.

There oughta be a law. Why? Because of my checkered past, of course.

My history with trucks is frightening. That's why God, in his infinite wisdom, has prevented me from purchasing an SUV. He's protecting all of you from my truck-driving eccentricities.

As a teenager fueling DC-10s at Philadelphia International in the '80s, I once drove a truck into an airplane. I know what you're thinking. How did he hit an airplane? Didn't he see it?

I saw the airplane. I just didn't see the wing.

I still remember the jolt of the truck and a coworker trying to wave me away from the plane--as if the 300 or so people onboard hadn't just watched what happened in horror from the windows.

I recall the panicked look in the pilot's eyes as he ran from the cockpit yelling, "Stoooophpp!"

But most of all I remember the next day, when the boss called me into his office and spoke in soothing tones.

"Tell me the truth," he said, as if he understood my plight. "It's okay."

Then, a few minutes later, in the same reassuring

voice, he fired me.

I was bitter. Still am. I have flashbacks about it every few years.

I think that's why every time I drive a truck somebody gets hurt. Problem is, more often than not, that somebody is me.

Last weekend's truck episode began innocently enough. I called and reserved a truck because we had to move a house full of stuff into storage while we shop for a new home.

Knowing my sorry truck history, I secretly hoped that something would go wrong. You know, the usual truck rental shenanigans.

"Oh, you wanted a 24-foot truck? I thought you said you wanted Peking Duck."

"I ain't say $89. That was Marvin Gaye in the background, singin' 'Make Me Wanna Holler.' The truck is $200, plus five bucks a mile, plus insurance, city tax, state tax, federal tax and thumb tacks. For a grand total of ... $1,000!"

Of course people never say stuff like that when you want them to. In fact, the Ryder people at Jim's Getty were especially helpful. They had the reservation ready, handed me the keys and wished me godspeed.

No special license. No background check. No questions about the infamous plane incident. Just a friendly smile and the keys to 10 tons o' diesel-fueled fun.

I walked outside with keys in hand and climbed onto the step that's right above the gas tank and right below the driver's seat. I figure they put the gas tank there so the fatal explosion can happen immediately after the crash.

As I contemplated this, LaVeta, who knows the awful truth about me and trucks (I think I was forced to divulge it in premarital counseling), took out an instant camera and snapped a picture of me behind the wheel.

I figured it was just as well. At least Eve would know how her daddy went on to Glory.

The rest of the day is something of a blur. I remember reading Moving Tip No. 12 on the side of one of the trucks that was parked in the lot as I pulled out.

It said, "Wear plenty of deodorant [for the move]." The words were accompanied by a stick figure holding a box, with squiggly stink lines emanating from its underarms.

I had unwittingly chosen not to follow that helpful tip, having already packed away the deodorant in one of our gazillion cardboard boxes. By day's end, I smelled like a trucker. I see now why they travel in such large vehicles. Cars can't contain that type of funk.

Wear plenty of deodorant [for the move] ... I had already chosen not to follow that tip.

Still, I survived. Despite my stinky underarms and the man-eating potholes on Washington Lane, despite the teenaged help that spent more time playing with the truck's hydraulic lift than lifting heavy items, despite the fact that I hit my knee so hard on a piece of furniture that I thought I'd never walk the steps of the Eagles new stadium this fall, I survived my latest truck-driving adventure.

Maybe now, after all these years, I can finally put the plane incident to rest.

Boogie Wonderland

Our new home held more than the usual surprises.

We recently bought our first home, but we haven't moved in yet, because we wanted to clean and paint the place first. And thank God. Because the things we discovered once we started to work on our new abode were so revolting, so utterly nasty, that they would make a slug cringe.

I'm not saying that the previous owners were triflin'. There may be a perfect explanation for the things we've seen. Perhaps, when realtors were showing the house to prospective buyers, they brought in a family that had been raised by wolves.

Or maybe some Vikings happened to swing through Mt. Airy right before we bought the place, and squatted at the house for a week or two. Or maybe, just maybe, the boogieman used to live there.

Because that's exactly what we've seen lining the otherwise pristine walls of our new home.

Boogies.

It all started when LaVeta went to the house one day last week and started to paint around the bottom of the kitchen counter. (That's right--my wife's not only fine, she paints, too.) Once she got close enough to apply the brush, she saw something on the wall. Something brown. And smeared. And disgusting.

"It was a boogie," she later told me. "It looked like it must have been an isolated incident where a kid sat at the counter and dug up their nose and wiped it on the wall, like some kids do at school."

LaVeta, being the trooper she is, put on gloves, cleaned the offending object from the wall with a bucket and disinfectant, then continued to paint. She rationalized it, figuring it was the kind of thing that kids do before being corrected by their parents.

But when LaVeta finished the kitchen and started upstairs, in the bedroom we're planning to use for Eve, there was more of the same.

"I saw maybe two, three at the most," she later told me.

Again, she cleaned the walls and painted. But she wasn't alarmed, because she could tell by the cartoon character on the light switch that the room had been occupied by a child. Kids do stuff like that. But adults don't.

At least that's what we thought. But we were wrong. Horribly, horribly wrong.

The day after the first few boogie sightings, I came home from work and accompanied LaVeta to the house so we could start on the master bedroom. I could tell as we drove to the house that there was something weighing on her. But I had no idea it was boogies.

We went into the master bedroom, and as I began to paint the ceiling, and she started to paint around the woodwork, I heard her say something like, "Eeeeew!"

That's right. She'd seen a boogie. And as she moved across the wall, painting around the rest of the woodwork, she saw more. Dozens more. That's when we both knew the boogies weren't just the work of children.

There were adults involved, as well.

"The boogies were up so high that I knew a child couldn't have done that," LaVeta later told me. "It had to be the work of an adult--someone at least 5-foot-5. The boogies were high up, like someone had raised their hand and wiped them across the wall."

We wiped off some, scraped off others, and some were so stubborn, so ground in, that they had to be painted over.

Asked how the discovery of the boogie problem

affected her, LaVeta didn't hesitate. "It made me feel that a chronic nosepicker once occupied this home," she said matter-of-factly. "But it makes me nauseous when I think about it, too."

Yeah, it's kind of sickening to me, as well. But like always, the Joneses will make the best of a bad situation.

In fact, we might even make it into a theme of sorts. So don't be surprised if, when you come to our housewarming, you hear Earth, Wind and Fire belting out their smash hit "Boogie Wonderland."

Feel free to dance. But please, don't wipe anything on the wall. 'Cause it ain't that type o' party.

Current Check-Outs summary for MONDELLO,
Sat Apr 06 13:01:49 CDT 2013

BARCODE: 31984002917399
TITLE: The last confession / Solomon Jon
DUE DATE: Apr 20 2013

BARCODE: 38510101608010
TITLE: Keeping up with the Jones / Solom
DUE DATE: Apr 20 2013

Kids

Waking LIfe

Since Eve was born, "it's" become a distant memory.

As I write this, it's 4:42 a.m. And I'm up thinking about the days when I would be in bed with LaVeta at this hour--doing it.

We'd do it on our sides. We'd do it on our backs. We'd even do it on our stomachs. No position was forbidden. And frankly, neither was any location.

We used to do it on my mother's couch, because it gave us plenty of room to maneuver. We almost did it a few times in public, but decided against it, because there were just too many people watching.

Back when we were young and free, in love with each other and in love with life, we were doing it so often that we had little time for anything else. But that all changed 16 months ago, when our daughter Eve--the screamer--was born.

So as I sit here in the dark, praying that my wife and I will someday get back to doing it on a regular basis, I guess the only thing I have left is memories. Memories of sleep. And the way we used to do it all night long.

In truth, we were doing it even before we were married. We had to see what it was like. I mean, suppose one of us was too noisy, or too wild, or had cold feet?

Happily, we found that we were compatible our very first time--when we did it on LaVeta's parents' couch.

We were watching the Million Dollar Movie, or something like that. But we were more interested in watching each other than seeing Dirty Harry make someone's day.

And so, as the television droned on, we cuddled. Our lips parted. Our eyes squeezed shut. Our breathing became heavy. Our hearts beat in sync. Though we didn't want to go further than that, we couldn't stop. Because when it's late, and it's quiet, and it's dark, you just can't help going all the way.

And so we did.

We slumbered right there on her mama's couch.

That first rendezvous led to another. Then another. And before we knew it, we were out of control.

We did it at my mom's house after big Sunday dinners. We did it on Thanksgiving and Christmas, after family gatherings. We nearly did it in the back of LaVeta's father's car when he was driving us home one day.

Fortunately, LaVeta's tendency to get motion sick stopped us from going that far.

By the time we were married and living in our own little apartment, we had it down to a regular routine. We'd go to work, come home, and in an extended explosion of forbidden pleasure, we'd do it all night long.

When it's late, and it's quiet, and it's dark, you just can't help going all the way.

We threw down a comforter and did it on the floor. We lowered our pleated shades and did it in the morning. We did it on the sofa bed when we wanted a change of pace. We even did it in a really big armchair from Ikea.

Talk about unböring.

But alas, about a year and three months into our marriage, our days of doing it ended abruptly. And it was all due to the birth of our daughter, Eve.

In her first few months with us, she developed all kinds of tricks to interrupt our routine.

She'd do ungodly things in her diaper and force us to clean up the mess. She'd get in our bed with us and form a little barrier. But mostly, she'd scream in the middle of the night.

Though Eve's shenanigans have decreased considerably, she still wakes up screaming. Last week she did it four times--at 4 in the morning.

Which means that these days, I wake up at 4 in the morning, too.

That's why I'm writing right now instead of doing it. That's why I'm sitting here, coming to terms with the fact that the magic is gone. That's why, on most days, no position or location--no matter how kinky--is good enough to bring back the ecstasy.

It doesn't matter if we try it on our backs, on our stomachs or on our sides; in our parents' homes, in the car or on the sofa bed. I'm not getting it nearly as much as I would like. And neither is LaVeta.

In fact, the only person in the Jones household who gets to sleep these days is Eve. For us, meanwhile, peaceful slumber has become a distant memory, and Eve is the only one who gets it.

In fact, she's in her crib right now, doin' sleep all by herself.

All About Eve

And the forbidden fruit . . . and hoagies . . . and cake.

There's an aggressive panhandler in my house. No, it's not one of the Center City regulars. Our panhandler is smaller, smarter, faster. A bionic panhandler, if you will.

At a compact two-and-a-half feet tall, she mouths unintelligible words and has a penchant for sneaking up on my wife and me during meals.

She doesn't use handwritten signs or battered cups to collect her loot. She uses weird screeching noises, signals like pointing and waving, and will resort to outright yelling if the grub comes her way too slowly.

Who is this person? It's Eve, my 14-month-old daughter. And she's dangerous. Deceptively so. Especially since she's begun growing molars, and with them, the ability to chew.

LaVeta and I blame ourselves for Eve's panhandling ways, because we're both greedy. I normally eat myself onto the floor at holiday gatherings. And LaVeta has food dreams. Sort of like the drug dreams addicts have, but with chocolate eclairs instead of illicit substances.

I admit it. We've got problems. I'm inhaling a Big 'N Tasty even as I write this column. But we can handle our food demons. We're adults. The question is, will the Jones genes prove too much for a baby whose food-panhandling habit is clearly out of control?

Our daughter's problem began to manifest itself six or seven months ago, when she had only, like, four teeth.

She'd be sitting by the kitchen table in her high chair at dinner time, happily eating Gerber chicken with rice, or oatmeal with bananas, or some other sliced-and-diced bland mush. Then she'd spot us with turkey, bacon, a sandwich or anything else that didn't look like baby food. And immediately she'd start in with the panhandling.

"Eeeeh!" she would scream, tossing aside her pureed baby stew.

We'd turn to find her reaching toward us, her eyes fixed in the bug-eyed stare of a food lunatic.

At first, we'd laugh and remark about how cute it was that she wanted table food. Then we'd turn back to our meals and continue to eat.

"Da-da! Da-da!"

She'd call me out. And when I would turn to look, I would find those big brown eyes staring up at me, bitterly accusing me of food betrayal.

Of course, I would relent. And as she would climb onto my lap and inhale my dinner, piece by tiny piece, it was almost like her lips would turn up into a got-you-sucker smile.

Things grew worse when Eve started going to my mother's house. We should have known it would happen, 'cause in the time-honored vernacular of black folks, my mom's food is so good, it tastes like she must've stuck her big toe in it.

Not that begging for my mother's food is entirely Eve's fault. LaVeta and I set the precedent for panhandling at Mom's. When we were dating, we would hang around on Sunday afternoons, never outwardly begging. Just sort of lingering near the dining room table until Mom fed us.

So when Eve started going to Grandmom's house on a regular basis, she just picked up where Mommy and Daddy left off.

Like her parents, she already knew how to lurk near the food. And when my mother started cooking around her, Eve would sort of crawl up to her ankles and stare up.

Being a grandmom, and thus intent on spoiling our child, my mom would give in. It's like she would forget all the little food hustles that she would catch my brother and me trying to run when we were growing up.

Nothing was off-limits for Eve. Not cake, not candy, not even fried chicken. She came back to our home having tasted the fruit of the forbidden tree. And she was determined to taste it again. And again.

Eve knows how to walk now, which means that eating chicken at the Jones residence is almost like having Jason from the *Friday the 13th* movies chasing you down.

There is no background noise going, "Chee-chee-chee-ha-ha-ha."

Eve makes her own background noise. It's called screaming.

And that's not her only panhandling weapon. She waves at us. She grins. She even kisses to get what she wants. And if all else fails, she sneaks.

That's how she got to the chocolate cake at the family Christmas brunch. While we sang "Silent Night," Eve took a silent right and ended up at the dessert table, smearing chocolate icing all over her face.

In desperation, we've taken to hiding. LaVeta stands in the kitchen, eating hoagies with her back turned. I sit in the car, polishing off Quarter Pounders with the engine running.

Most of the time, in spite of our best efforts, Eve catches us. And when she does, we reward her panhandling prowess with forbidden morsels.

So there. It's out. My daughter's a food panhandler. And she's darn good at it. She should be. She learned it from the best.

Eve Wants An F-150

Who cares if she's still in Pull-Ups?

Last week a friend asked me to identify Eve's big Christmas gift. I told him there was no real big-ticket item this Christmas. Eve got a bunch of small stuff, because she's not into the toy thing yet, and in truth, I doubt she ever will be.

She's a lot like her parents. She doesn't want big stuff. She wants *really* big stuff. And she has no money.

While other 2-year-old girls were watching TV commercials and pointing to Hokey Pokey Elmo and the Powerpuff Girls this past Christmas, Eve had her sights set on a gift I'd never dreamed of.

Maybe she was smitten by the country music playing in the background, or the pompom-wielding Swedish bikini team girls, or the fat dude in the drive-through window daydreaming about getting one. But when Eve saw the commercials for the Dodge Ram Truck, she fell in love. And like any love-struck girl, she gleefully pointed to the object of her desire and said the magic words.

"Eve's car!"

Horrified, I tried to discourage her. I told her that Eve's car--a sensible foreign number--was parked outside our house. And while she understood that concept and acknowledged that the car outside was indeed hers, she never wavered from her insistence that the Dodge Ram was hers, too.

I thought it would end there. Unfortunately, it didn't.

The Chevy truck commercials had the same effect. In fact, the effect may have been even worse. I think it was because of the song. You know the one. It goes something like this:

"Like a rock, I was strong as I could be. Like a rock. Nothing ever got to me."

Of course, Eve is more like a marshmallow than a rock. She likes really girly stuff--from makeup and clothes to dollies in strollers.

But when you show her a pickup truck, she's transformed from an Elmo-watching toddler to John Wayne in Pull-Ups. Her fondness for lilting cowboy melodies with slide guitar riffs is apparently a part of that.

But I've gotta break her. No daughter of mine's gonna be some country-singin', cattle-rustlin', pickup-drivin', gun-totin' cowgirl.

So the next time the Ford F-150 commercial comes on, and my daughter points to the screen and says, "Eve's car!" I'm gonna lay down the law.

"Honey," I'll say, with a tight, disingenuous smile. "That's not your car. Your car's outside."

She'll look at me, point to the screen and repeat her mantra.

"Eve's car!"

"Eve, your car is outside. It's not a pickup, and besides, you don't have a driver's license, and your feet can't reach the pedals."

She'll look at me, with lips quivering and eyes watering, and she'll cry out in that tortured little helpless voice that girls use to manipulate their daddies.

"Eve's car!"

And that's when I'll finally give in.

To get a jump on my baby's pickup fixation, I plan to open one of those Christmas savings accounts this week. And then, in preparation for the big purchase this year, I plan to take Eve on a tour of Dodge, Chevy and Ford dealerships.

I have nothing against Japanese cars--I have one, in fact. But when you're going the pickup route, you can't go foreign. You've got to go American. And you've got to go all the way.

And so, before we go out to test-drive Eve's Ford F-150--complete with gun rack, roll bar and winch--I will purchase every accessory she needs to be a true pick-up aficionado.

I'll get her a two-disc set of Conway Twitty's greatest hits, denim pants, a denim Onesie, denim Pull-Ups and a really big Stetson hat with a picture of Elmo on the side. I'll pay for her initial membership in the National Rifle Association, and get her some steer-roping lessons. And because I want her to be able to relax with her pickup-drivin' colleagues when she's chillin' at truck stops, I'll teach her to whittle.

Yes, I'm gonna support my daughter in her quest to become a pickup-truck owner. But I will temper her adult-sized ambitions with little reminders of childhood.

Her truck's horn will be programmed to play the Sesame Street tune. Her cowboy boots will have Mickey Mouse ears on the sides. And the first speed-dial number on her little pink truck phone will be Daddy's.

Just in case she ever needs me to send AAA.

There's The Rub

Everything's better with Vaseline.

My mother loves to tell the story of the time she left the Vaseline too close to my crib. I was about 18 months old, I guess, and I was supposed to be taking a nap. But with Vaseline nearby, sleeping was not an option.

And so while Mom was downstairs, I reached between the bars of my crib and grabbed it.

By the time my unsuspecting mother came upstairs, I had covered my body, slathered the bars of my crib, greased the walls of my room and coated the sheets with Vaseline.

Now it looks like my 18-month-old daughter, Eve, is a Vaseline-head, too.

It's gotten so bad that we can't leave petroleum jelly on anything less than 4 feet high. If we do, Eve will take it down, remove the cap, slather it on her chin, hands and hair, then rub it on everyone's clothes, thus doing permanent, oily damage.

Given my greasy history, you may think that Eve's Vaseline obsession is strictly hereditary. But it's much more than that. It's cultural.

Because in North Philly, where I come from, Vaseline is like penicillin.

It's the cure for whatever ails you.

Take ash, for example. What's ash, you say? It's the stuff that makes your skin look like you've been attacked by powder-wielding thugs. Still don't know what it is? Look at your elbows. Are they white and dry? Congratulations! You're ashy.

That's not such a big deal nowadays. With the newfound tolerance that's come with political correctness, ashy people are free to roam about in all their gray-skinned glory.

But when I was coming up in the oppressive era of ash discrimination, I saw ashy people brought to tears by the cruel taunts of others.

"Your mom feet so ashy she look like she been walkin' in flour!"

"You mom lips so ashy they look like a pair o' jelly donuts!"

And woe to the ashy person who was without Vaseline. Because if they lived where I lived, they couldn't afford Neutrogena, Eucerin or Lubriderm. Not that such lubricants make a difference in the war on ash. They don't. No lotion, no matter how fancy, removes ash like the big V.

That's why ash laughs in the face of lotion. Because ash, when it's really bad, is almost as tough as foot crust--that stuff that can be scraped or chiseled away only with stones and razors. And to fight ash, you need lubricating power that lasts.

You need Vaseline. Because putting lotion on ash is like putting Peter McNeeley in the ring with Mike Tyson. The fight lasts for about 30 seconds, and nobody wants to see the rematch.

Of course, ash removal is just one common use for Vaseline. There are other uses, too.

Before Chapstick and Blistex, Vaseline made it possible to treat dangerous crusty lips. Some people ignore that use, as evidenced by the annual proliferation of chapped, nasty lips in winter and summer. But for those who want to be helped, Vaseline means never having to interrupt a kiss to say, "I'm sorry I cut you with my dried-out knifelike lips."

It's not just about personal safety, either. Vaseline has other grooming advantages, as well.

In the '70s and '80s, if you couldn't afford Afro

Sheen, Royal Crown or any of that other hair goop, Vaseline allowed the common man to have a hairstyle that could compete.

For black guys, a little Vaseline was the alternative to the latest Don Cornelius Soul Train pitch. For white guys, Vaseline was the cheap way to look like the Fonz.

For all of us, it was, and is, so much more.

Got a rusty bike chain? Vaseline! Door hinges jammed? The big V. Don't want to get scratched in a catfight? Vaseline! (Okay, ladies, maybe you should avoid catfights in the first place, but don't try to act like you never saw Vaseline used for that.)

The point is, there's nothing in this world that's cheaper and has so many uses as the greasy stuff. And if my little Eve has already discovered its virtues, just as I did when I was her age, well, I'm proud of her.

As long as she keeps a little Vaseline by her side, I know she'll be all right.

No Problem

Eve has years to practice the magic word.

I'm married, so my wife tells me "no." I have a mom. She still tells me "no." I try to sell book and movie ideas to people, and female publishers and producers tell me "no."

Being the happy-go-lucky guy I am, I try not to let the rejection affect me. And for the most part it doesn't.

But each "no" I hear from a woman brings back memories of every "no" I used to get when I was a kid. Especially from girls.

"Can I get a kiss?"

"No."

"How about a hug?"

"No."

"A date?"

"With you? No!"

With my history, hearing ladies say "no" brings back all kinds of hurt, and opens up all kinds of wounds.

So last week when my daughter, Eve, said "no" to me for the first time, I was taken aback. Even a little injured.

Then it hit me. She's a female. And females derive their power from a single word: "no."

At 19 months Eve hasn't mastered many words. She's pretty much limited to mama, dada, amen and hallelujah (yes, she's a church baby). But she's got the pantomime thing down pat.

Blowing a kiss means "goodbye." Pointing to something while whimpering means "gimme that." Grabbing Daddy's leg when we're out in public means "I'm scared." And shaking her head from side to side when we try to give her stuff means "no."

She did the "no" thing the other night when I tried to give her a piece of fried chicken. Which was strange to me, because if you're in the Jones clan, you love the fried stuff.

Knowing Eve's genetic predisposition to KFC, Popeyes, Church's and most other varieties of cooked fowl, I ignored her little display, and tried to hand it to her again.

More head-shaking, then a raised hand. Sort of like she was saying, "Feed the hand, cause the mouth ain't eatin' that chicken."

"Is she saying 'no'?" I asked my wife, who was sitting there, clearly amused.

"Yes, she is."

At that point, the two of them exchanged a look. Not mother-to-daughter, but woman-to-woman. I didn't understand it then. But I do now.

By refusing that piece of chicken, and saying "no" to a man for the very first time, Eve had completed a rite of passage. And the look she exchanged with LaVeta meant she'd been inducted into the Secret Society of the "No" Sisters.

By saying 'no' to a man for the first time, Eve had completed a rite of passage.

Eve's membership in that society means that from this point forward her power over males will increase by the day.

In the next year or so, little boys will ask to share her graham crackers. She will cruelly refuse them. In four years they will ask her to play house. She will laugh derisively. In six years they will ask her for kisses. And she will crush their hearts with a single two-letter word: "no."

This childhood cruelty, which is wholly appropriate when dealing with little boys, will carry over nicely into adolescence, where Eve will have to be even more skillful in her use of the n-word.

You see, when boys grow into teenagers, they become giant walking hormones. No faces, no legs, no torsos. Just big blobs of nastiness in search of one thing: a naive little girl who has not been inducted into the Secret Society of the "No" Sisters.

Because Eve will have already had years of practice by the time she reaches adolescence, she will know what to do when these filthy boys approach her and begin their disgusting line of questioning.

"Can I get a kiss?"

"No."

"How about a hug?"

"No."

"A date?"

"With you? No!"

If they amble away with their hearts in traction, permanently damaged by the rejection, as I have been over the years, she will have done her job. And the boys will someday look back with bitterness and hurt.

If they choose to stay and try to get to know her beyond the word "no," well, they might just be worthy of a conversation.

Anything beyond that, and they're asking for a visit from Daddy. And by the time I finish with them, I guarantee they'll know what the word "no" means.

'Cause they'll be screaming it at the top of their lungs.

Pigskin Predictions

My daughter is learning the joys of bupbaw.

Labor Day's gone and summer's over. Unlike many of you, I can face that, because my life doesn't change dramatically during summer. I'm a dad and a husband.

I go to work. I come home. I hand out money. That's my life. No matter the season.

Sure, I'll miss the summer weather, the long days, the water ice, the ice cream. But I won't miss the people. Because, frankly, summer is the season when most folks lose their minds.

Teenage girls believe every day above 80 degrees is an audition opportunity for a Nelly video. Little kids on skateboards try X Games tricks in rush-hour traffic. Men who've spent the last 20 years in easy chairs try crossover dribbles. And end up in traction.

Me? I know my limitations. I stick to my pushups, which keep me in denial as my arms harden and my stomach expands. And I limit my outdoor activity to short walks--usually from the parking lot to the mall entrance, or from the curb to the nearest cheesesteak place.

Summer has its place, but not for workaday saps like me whose lives are sucked away by car notes, mortgages, life insurance and home improvement.

Only autumn matters to guys like me. Because this is the time of year when we gather on Sunday afternoons and Monday nights to have conniptions over a meaningless game.

That's right, ladies and gentlemen. Summer is over. And now comes the only season that matters--football season.

Every year around this time the women in my life begin

to tease me, hoping to break the hold that football--specifically Eagles football--has on me. My mother will harp on the Eagles' propensity for losing the Big One. The Raiders Super Bowl loss. The Chicago Fog Bowl massacre. The NFC championship game whippings.

My wife will start mentioning the football-related changes in my behavior. Calling me rude for refusing to stand around and talk after Sunday church service. Claiming I'm insensitive for demanding silence during the radio broadcast on the ride home. Deriding my focus on the television on Sunday afternoons.

I'm not saying their accusations are false. I'm just saying they don't have to keep making them. I've already admitted that NFL football is, indeed, my mistress. And like the adulterous Kobe Bryant, I'll have to answer for that one day. Just don't let that day be Sunday. Or Monday night. Or Thursday, especially if there's a game on.

Just leave me alone for the three hours it will take for me to watch the game in its entirety. And if the Eagles lose, walk away slowly, and don't come back until I grunt.

When I grunt, I'm ready to talk. But not about football. Home repair, maybe.

Fortunately, some women like football. And I'm not just talking about cheerleaders. There are real women who understand the role of football in maintaining male sanity.

There are knowledgeable female sideline reporters at most sports networks. Female fans go to the games. And then there are girls like my daughter, Eve, who I'm training to occupy my butt groove on the couch when I go on to that great football field in the sky.

That's right. Along with regular 2-year-old stuff like potty training, numbers and the alphabet, I'm teaching Eve the intricacies of the Two Deep Zone, the Zone

Blitz and the West Coast Offense. Don't tell my wife, but I've actually slipped a little sheet of plays into one of her children's books.

When I turn on the television, our football lessons begin in earnest.

"Eve, what are those guys in helmets doing?"

"Bupbaw!"

"How about those guys running around the bases?"

"Bupbaw!"

"And the guys bouncing that orange ball?"

"Bupbaw!"

Doesn't matter that she doesn't know the difference between the sports yet. As long as she understands that football is the only one that counts, she'll be okay.

She's already wearing her own little butt groove into the couch, and she's mastered the art of eating popcorn and watching television at the same time. She claps after almost every play, and follows my lead whenever I cheer.

Next week I plan to let her hold the remote control. To get the feel of it in her hands, and understand the power. If she can handle that responsibility, then she will be ready for her final gift: an Eagles jersey.

That, along with an understanding of the game, will someday spare her husband and children from the grief I've had to bear all these years.

Yes, ladies and gentlemen, I'm raising my daughter up right. And I'm preparing her for the only season that matters--bupbaw season.

With Flying Colors

A pink fluffy plaything poses the toughest test of my manhood.

I've done all kinds of things to prove my manhood. I've had fistfights. I've dated lots of women. I even joined the Marine Corps, where I rappelled down the side of a tower, stood still while sand fleas chewed my butt, and endured the cruel taunts of a drill instructor who told me I marched like a Mummer.

I boxed as a youth, though I quit after about a year because I couldn't imagine why anyone--especially me--would volunteer to be beaten about the head and neck.

But nothing has tested my manhood like being the father of a 2-year-old girl.

I've been handed clip-on earrings to try on (for the record, I refused to do so). I've been called upon to rock baby dolls. And in Queer Eye for the Straight Guy-type moments, I've been forced to color-coordinate ensembles plucked from among the hundreds of dresses and skirts our relatives have purchased for Eve.

Don't get me wrong. I'm cool with it. It's cute. That's why, when my wife bought Eve a little pink phone decorated with sequins, feathers and a heart in the middle of the musical dial pad, I was prepared to do my duty.

Well, sort of.

"Hewwo?" Eve grabs the feather-laden phone and dials up Mom-Mom.

After coming home from work, where I spent the day fighting the good fight, I've just sat down to dinner. It's late, so Eve and LaVeta have already eaten. I'm alone at the table, and there's only one piece of chicken between me and the phone. I hurriedly bite into it, hoping that the distraction will keep me out of the conversation.

"Hi Mom-Mom!" Eve says happily.

My mother isn't answering. I know it. Eve knows it. It's a toy phone. Nobody answers. But that's not stopping Eve from edging closer to me, holding out the little pink phone in the hope that I, too, will allow my imagination to run wild.

"Dada?"

She looks up at me with those big hopeful eyes, and I do something no human being has ever been able to make me do. I put down my chicken. Then I take the phone and raise it to my ear.

Since the feathers kinda tickle, I adjust the phone so that it's farther back off my ears. A couple of the tiny feathers catch on the razor stubble that sprouts from my shaved head. I'm wondering if it looks like a Mae West boa.

"Dada!" Eve points to the phone. "Mom-Mom!" she says, insisting that I get in on the conversation.

"Hi Mom," I say hesitantly. "How are you?"

As I say this, a feather shakes loose from the phone and Eve smiles ear to ear.

LaVeta suddenly snaps a picture. Me: big, black and bald. The phone: frilly, feathery and cute. I wonder if the guys at One-Hour Photo will understand.

Since then, I've had numerous conversations with various relatives on the pink feather phone. I've resolved family issues that we could never deal with on a regular phone, what with all the bugging going on these days. I've laughed and joked with relatives I haven't spoken to in years.

In fact, I've learned to embrace the pink phone, partly because it reminds me of one of Eve's favorite books, *ABC* by Dr. Seuss, where the letter "F" is represented by four fluffy feathers on a fiffer-feffer-feff.

But more than that, the phone reminds me that

these days, when my daughter wants to talk to me, wants to watch football with me, wants to sit on my lap and hear about the fiffer-feffer-feff, will someday come to an end.

Twelve years from now she'll cringe at the thought of my picking out her clothes, or playing with her phone, or reading silly stories to her. She'll be looking to become her own person, to make her own mistakes, to carve out her own identity.

And right about then, I'll look back at the picture of that bald black man with the little pink phone, and I'll long for days like these.

Eve of Destruction

If we don't keep our daughter safe, Mom mom's gonna get us.

The other day a co-worker asked me Eve's clothing size. "I don't know," I said, offhandedly. "My mom buys all her clothes."

And she does. Eve's first pair of patent leather shoes? Mom-mom Carol. Her first and only pair of Timberland boots? Mom-mom again. The half-dozen jackets and coats with matching hats and gloves? You got it. Mom-mom Carol.

Not that I mind my mother doing special things for Eve. In fact, I'd like to encourage her to continue her Mom-mom duties well into Eve's adulthood. The prom? Mom-mom. First car? Mom-mom. And if I can't cajole, harass, torment and pester Eve into earning an academic scholarship for college, well, Mom-mom, you know what to do.

But it's not just about money (which is a good thing, because none of us is rich). It's really about my mother exercising her God-given right to spoil our daughter rotten, to love her beyond comprehension, and to let her get away with all the things my brother and I couldn't have dreamed of when we were kids.

Which brings me to the point of this story. My mother, the doting grandmother who loves little Eve in every way possible, and cuts her slack whenever she gets the chance, doesn't give us the same kind of breaks. In fact, she's threatened to do bodily harm to both me and LaVeta if anything ever happens to Eve.

Well, something happened. And I've been hiding Eve from my mother ever since.

It all started last Sunday when we came home from church. The Eagles weren't playing, so my weird, fanatical relationship with football was off for the day. I had run out of excuses concerning the fallen leaves in front of our house, and hoping that they'd disappear was just not working.

To add to the day's weirdness, LaVeta, who had recently discovered a boutique supermarket that sold pumpkin-flavored ice cream, became convinced that spice cookies were the only adequate complement to this strange autumn delicacy.

Though I had promised to take her to the market after raking the leaves, she couldn't wait. So with obsessive-compulsive food tendencies in tow, she served a great dinner, cleared our plates, then ran out the door to satisfy her cookie jones.

Not a problem. Eve and I would rake the leaves together. It would be fun.

I dressed Eve in one of her Mom-mom-Carol coats (with matching hat, of course) and hustled her out the door with a rake, a broom, a dustpan and some trash bags.

And just as I thought, it was fun. Right up until Eve took the rake, which I'd repeatedly tried to keep upright and out of the way, and laid it down on the sidewalk. She then tripped over it and fell flat on her face, chipping her tooth and scraping her nose.

If the rake had been a person, I'd have punched it. But since it wasn't, I just punched myself. Then I took Eve inside, iced her swelling lip, put antibiotic ointment on her scratches, and waited for LaVeta to come home with the cookies.

"Your mother's gonna kill me," I said to Eve, again and again.

But what I really meant was, Mom-mom Carol's gonna kill us both.

That Monday we took Eve to the dentist, where she screamed bloody murder while he tried to repair her tooth.

"You have to sit still, Eve!" I said in frustration. Dr. Moody, our dentist, reminded me that she's only 2.

Duly chastised, I gave the kid a break. But in reality, my frustration wasn't with Eve. I was frustrated with myself. If only I'd watched a little closer, or kept her on the grass, or stayed in the house, or driven LaVeta for cookies, we wouldn't be facing the death penalty at the hands of Mom-mom Carol.

But hey, what's a guy to do? I can only hope that by the time my mom reads this, Eve's scratches will be healed, and my wife and I will not have to perish.

But in case they're not, and LaVeta and I disappear, I want everyone to know that it wasn't the butler.

The Mom-mom did it.

Potty Mouth

When all else fails, try "Peepee Doodoo."

Lately, when my daughter Eve sees us gathering her toys, turning out lights and checking the door locks downstairs, she correctly deduces that bedtime is imminent.

And that's when the excuses begin.

"Ooosh!" she says urgently. In Eve-speak, this means she wants juice.

When we accommodate this request, she moves on to phase two.

"Nack!" she says, looking up at us with those pitiful 2-year-old eyes.

I'm a sucker for that look. Eve knows it. But I have to be strong.

"No snacks," I say in my authoritative daddy voice. "It's bedtime."

Eve starts to whine as I pick her up and carry her up the stairs and along the proverbial Green Mile that leads to the bathroom. We brush her teeth, wash her face and sit her on the potty. She doesn't do anything there, so we take her into her room, say her prayers with her and tuck her in.

For the next few moments, it's quiet. Then Eve moves on to phase three.

"Peepee doodoo!" she shouts.

And that's when she has us. Because peepee doodoo isn't just a free return trip to the potty. It's the ultimate excuse for everything.

Workplace drama

You've been late to work every day for the past month. You're three weeks behind on a project that should've taken an hour, and you've been stealing staples, notepads and pens from the office supply closet since you were hired.

Though common sense should tell you that your day of reckoning is coming, you're still telling yourself that you're indispensable.

Maybe that's why, when two guys from security stop at your desk to accompany you out of the building, you're caught totally off-guard.

As they stand ominously over your shoulder, you think frantically back to the list of your best excuses. "I think I hear my mother calling me," you say, using the line that helped you avoid a fight or two when you were a kid.

"Your mother's not here," says one of the security guards. "Clean out your desk."

"I, uhh, think the dog ate my homework," you say, trembling nervously.

"You don't get homework here," says the other guard. "Let's go."

As they snatch you from your seat and start dragging you down the hall, it hits you.

"Peepee doodoo!" you scream.

At that moment, everything stops. Because no one can deny you a trip to the potty. Even when you're being fired and escorted from the building.

Relationship troubles

You've been cheating on your significant other from day one. But now you're broke, because you recently lost your job. And to make matters worse, your partner is none other than J. Lo.

Knowing her track record with men, especially broke ones, you've been avoiding her requests to talk to you. When she finally catches you at one of your favorite clubs, surrounded by your boys, your first instinct is to play the tough role. But you saw her in that movie *Enough*, and you don't want to chance getting a beat-down in front of your friends.

You're trapped. You know it. And you really need an excuse to avoid this conversation.

"I, uhh, don't think this is a good time to talk," you say evasively.

Your boys, who never believed you could hold onto J. Lo anyway, look at you with self-satisfied smirks.

"This won't take long," she says, tapping her foot impatiently.

As the smirks turn into full-fledged laughter, you make the only excuse that has never failed you.

"Peepee doodoo!" you yell.

The music goes silent. Your boys stop laughing. Even J. Lo gives you a pass. Because if a grown man has to resort to peepee doodoo, he's been humiliated enough already.

Of course there are other situations when nothing but the trump card will work.

Got a drug or alcohol problem, and your family and friends have you surrounded for an intervention? Peepee doodoo.

In boot camp and preparing to jump out of a plane to get your airborne wings, but forgot to tell the sergeant that you're scared of heights? Peepee doodoo.

Getting ready to defend your doctoral thesis before a university review board, but you plagiarized the whole thing? Peepee doodoo.

Seventy-years-old with a 24-year-old girlfriend, but you forgot your Viagra? You got it. Peepee doodoo.

Yep, Eve has given me countless hours of fun, lots of great memories and a few good scares over the past two years. But in my estimation, one of the best things she's given me has been the trump card.

Peepee doodoo. It's not just for bedtime anymore.

Mirror Mirror

Need an incentive to be good? Try living with a 2-year-old mimic.

Whenever I'm talking about Bush, racism or some other insane aspect of my daily existence, I always finish my tirade with the words, "It's kinda deep."

The other day we were riding somewhere in the car. I'd just finished one of my rants, and said, "It's kinda ... "

Before I could complete my catchphrase, Eve, my 2-year-old, took her thumb out of her mouth, strained forward in her car seat and chimed in with the word "... deep."

I wasn't sure that I'd heard her correctly, so I looked at LaVeta, who'd missed the whole thing.

I then repeated the words, "It's kinda ... "

"Deep!" Eve shouted, before settling back into her seat with her thumb in her mouth.

LaVeta and I exchanged a terrified look, because this latest incident confirmed what we'd suspected for some time.

We've got a new mirror in the house. It weighs 30 pounds, stands 3 feet tall, and talks and eats a lot.

Our mirror mimics everything we do, even when we're not standing in front of it. Shame is, with this mirror, we can't dim the lights and make the blemishes go away.

Most of the time it's not that bad. When she was 1 we took her to one of our favorite seafood restaurants and gave her a little plate of fries and fish sticks. Not to be outdone by our shrimp-dippin', she started dipping her fries into her cole slaw.

In church she hears us say "amen" and "hallelujah," and does us one better: She waves her hands in the air when the choir sings.

But we, like everyone else, have our dark sides. And like all parents with little mirrors, we're just waiting for Eve to reflect them. My guess? She'll probably start by walking up to someone we've laughed about in private and let them in on the joke.

"Hi, Ms. Sadie," she'll say with her trademark grin. "My daddy says you smell like a wet dog."

An embarrassed smile will spread across my face.

"Didn't you say that, Daddy?"

As the subject of Eve's ill- advised outburst looks at me accusingly, I'll try--and fail--to lie about it.

"I, uh ... What I meant to say is that you smell like a hot dog. A really good hot dog. With mustard."

Of course, it hasn't gotten to that point yet. Right now the impersonations are still cute.

The other day, while trying to pilfer cheese curls from the utility closet we've converted into a snack treasure trove, Eve stood on her little chair and, unable to reach the object of her desire, went into LaVeta mode.

"Help me Jesus," she strained, while reaching for the cheese curls.

"Help me, Jesus," she strained, while reaching for the cheese curls. "Help me!"

He did. He sent LaVeta to get the cheese curls for her.

Still, our little mirror continues to reflect other things, as well. And the reflections ain't always pretty.

Eve's already making this strange growling sound that both LaVeta and I make when we're frustrated about something. She's also taken to mimicking all the stuff my wife says to her when she does something wrong.

"Get on my nerves," she says haltingly, her high-pitched voice accompanied by a furrowed brow and saucy attitude.

When she does this at home, we can correct her. But it's different when we're in public.

"Mate me an-gy," she said to me the other evening, while we were walking through the produce aisle at the supermarket.

It took me a few seconds to decipher what she'd meant.

"Are you saying something makes you angry?"

"Yeah!"

Excited that I'd broken the secret toddler code, I went a step further. "What makes you angry, Eve?"

"Daddy mate me an-gy!"

A lady sorting through the celery nearby stopped in her tracks and looked down at Eve with a bewildered look on her face. Then she moved slowly away from the two of us, apparently spooked by the fact that Eve is so in touch with her feelings.

I'm not sure there's anything we can do to keep our little mirror from going outside and showing the world our true reflection. So I guess we'll just have to take precautions to make sure our reflection is worth seeing.

The way I see it, there are a few things we can do to make sure that happens. We can go through life faking everything, so that Eve becomes our little *Stepford* child. We can show Eve one thing, and whenever she's out of sight, do another. Or we can do our best to make sure that we show her how we want her to act, rather than telling her.

I think we'll opt for No. 3.

And by the way, Sadie--you *do* smell like a wet dog. I'm telling you now, because I'd rather have you hear it from me, and not my little mirror.

United Colors of Babydom

Kids don't care what their friends look like . . . they're wise.

We were at dinner the other night, sitting in one of those booths they have at the chain restaurants. You know the type of booth I'm talking about. It's so close to the next one that you can reach over and smack your neighbor in the head.

Anyway, we were sitting there waiting for our food to arrive when a little boy in the next booth noticed Eve. With little action figures in hand, he smiled at her and waved his toys. She smiled back, pointed at him and said, "Boy!"

He didn't say much more, though he continued to lean over the back of his chair to catch glimpses of Eve. She happily acknowledged his overtures, and if we weren't eating (or anticipating eating, since our food took forever to arrive) I'm sure she would have begged us to play with him.

In fact, I'm sure she would have begged to play with the other two boys who were seated in a booth across from us. She'd spotted them as well. One of them looked to be about 2 years old, and the other may have been 5. They were giving their parents fits.

"Kids!" Eve said, while I watched the boys' father trying unsuccessfully to convince the 2-year-old to eat more macaroni and cheese and fewer french fries.

"That's right, honey," I said, marveling at her openness. "They're kids."

I marveled because, in Eve's mind, and indeed, in all four children's minds, all of them were just kids. It didn't matter that the first little boy was Asian, or that the other two boys were white, or that Eve was black.

What mattered to them was that they were kids. They had that much in common. Well, that and the fact that at least three of them were probably wearing Pull-Ups and fighting the urge to wet themselves.

I think everyone should be able to get along like that. And so, in an effort to solve the racial strife that seems to plague everyone past the age of 10 or so, I'm offering the following suggestions to help us all be more childlike.

Wear Pull-Ups

I know that most of you think you're past the potty training stage. And in most cases, you probably are. But I think that if everybody had to wear Pull-Ups, with that tight elastic that digs into your thighs, and that plastic that makes you sweat in your most personal space, no one would be comfortable enough to be racist.

Who has time to be bigoted when a plastic wedgie is an ever-present reality? Who can be biased so long as the specter of peeing oneself is hanging over one's head? Who can be oppressive when he's carrying a heavy load in the seat of his pants? No one.

I mean, if you were sitting in an important business meeting with some people from another culture, and you were wearing Pull-Ups, what do you think you'd be more concerned about? Your preconceived notions about them? Or the possibility that they might smell the funk emanating from your Pull-Ups?

I think we all know the answer to that question.

Carry Toys Wherever You Go

Wanna strike up a conversation with someone who's different from you? Toys are the ultimate ice-breaker.

Use them at work.

"Hey, Bob, how's that report coming along?"

"I didn't do it, Mr. Ali, but I've got a yo-yo that I've been dying to try out. Wanna play?"

"I thought you'd never ask."

Use them in restaurants.

"You know, waiter, I have no idea what the French words on this menu mean, and I'm not so sure about the size of the $150 portions, but I'll tell you what: If I can beat you in a game of *Madden 2004*, can you get the chef to hook up some chicken, collard greens and cornbread?"

"You're on, monsieur."

Use them at nightclubs.

"Hey Laqueesha, I like the way you move, but I can't dance like you. So tell you what: Instead of dancing to this 50 Cent song, let's play Twister."

"Ooh, Bif, you so crazy!"

Speak Gibberish

Toddlers get along because they can't understand the words they speak to each other. They don't have to worry about racist language. They only have to worry about body language. They cry when they're dissatisfied. They whine when they're being manipulative. They laugh when they're happy.

Maybe if adults would learn to speak gibberish, we wouldn't have to worry about racist language either. If we depended totally on body language to communicate, we could say what we mean, and mean what we say.

We could talk to anyone, play with anyone, even draw with anyone. And the only colors we'd have to worry about would be the shades of our crayons.

Fatherhood

Shirt Happens

How I hid the awful truth from Brandy: a father's confession.

I belong to an exclusive club called the Fatherhood Society. That means I get to work like a dog to support my family.

Some Society members get an extra bonus. They star in a reality show called *Baby Mama Drama*. It's on five days a week down at Family Court and features one poor slob after another getting jacked for half his check.

I appear on another reality show. It's called *Broke Man*. A typical story line goes something like this: Solomon pays household bills, eventually college tuition, then wedding expenses, and finally, a whole bunch of miscellaneous costs for grown children.

At the end of the show Solomon dies.

You know why? Because Solomon's a dad. And dads are there to provide for their families--not for themselves.

I know the drill. But I actually think there are times I can flip the script and do something for myself. I can be dense that way.

When my wife LaVeta and I were recently invited to a gala to benefit a nonprofit charity founded by Brandy and her husband, I decided to violate a club rule.

I got something for myself.

I figured even a dad should be able to get a new shirt and tie when he's meeting someone like Brandy, right?

I saw daylight the day of the gala, when LaVeta told me she wanted to go to Macy's to buy a new outfit for the event.

I owed LaVeta. Just two weeks earlier, to prove she was serious about saving money, she'd bought two pairs of bobos.

She wanted a new outfit, and I was all for her getting it.

We loaded our daughter Eve into the car for the drive to the mall. Along the way I began fixating on how I would--insert ominous musical progression here--buy something for myself.

"That's insane!" said my daddy self.

"No, it's not," said my before children self.

"But you'll be broke," the daddy voice said.

LaVeta, sitting next to me, must have sensed my inner turmoil.

"What are you thinking about, honey?" she asked.

"Nothing," I said, and patted her leg reassuringly.

But it was hardly nothing. I was about to break ranks with the Fatherhood Society.

The nondaddy voice grew louder as I waited with Eve while LaVeta tried on sequined tops and velour pants.

Eve started getting antsy, so I took her out of her baby carriage. She immediately began walking up and down the aisles, reaching up toward the racks, touching one garment, deciding against it, before moving onto something else.

"Buy something now, before it's too late!" the nondaddy voice implored.

When LaVeta came out of the dressing room and paid for her stuff, I blurted it out.

"I want to go up to the men's department and get a shirt and tie," I said. I tried to make it sound like a perfectly normal request.

LaVeta helped me pick out a wheat-colored silk shirt with the right neck size--and a matching tie. The whole thing came to just over $50.

But by the time we were through getting checked out at the register, we were running late for the gala. We hustled home and changed into our respective outfits.

When I put on my shirt, I knew right away something was wrong.

"Look, LaVeta!" I exclaimed.

The sleeves were 5 inches too short.

"What are you going to do?" she asked.

I put on my suit jacket and grabbed my car keys.

"What do you think I'm gonna do?" I said. "I'm gonna wear it and pray I don't have to take off this jacket."

You've heard of the old chitlin' circuit play, *Your Arms Too Short to Box With God* ?

I was getting ready to star in an all-new production. It was called *Your Sleeves Too Short to Eat with Brandy.*

When we got there, Brandy and her husband were already working the room, thanking people for contributing to their foundation.

As the event grew more crowded, it got a little warm. LaVeta and I huddled together, whispering.

It may have looked like we were lovey-dovey, exchanging sweet nothings in the corner.

But it was really about the shirt.

"You can make it, baby," she said.

"Can't ... take ... much ... more," I grimaced.

And I couldn't. But with her encouragement, I made it through, short long-sleeves and all.

When I got home, I renewed my vows to the Fatherhood Society. There'll be no more new stuff for me. No more listening to that pre-dad voice. I've learned my lesson. It's just not okay for dads to shop for things for themselves.

There'll be no more of that.

I hope my peers will forgive my temporary lapse in judgment. If they'll permit me, I'd like to come back and resume my recurring roles on *Broke Man.*

To demonstrate my contrition, I'll even wear my new shirt.

December Babies Unite!

We want our birthday reparations

Like everyone else born in December, I'm about to be screwed. Again.

Every year around this time I'm handed a couple of envelopes or gift boxes, accompanied by tight smiles and the words, "Here are your birthday presents. And your Christmas presents. Think of them as combo gifts."

I mumble thanks while opening the gifts. But I know I'm being shortchanged. And I'm tired of being nice about it.

I want separate Christmas and birthday gifts, just like the June babies, the February babies and the August babies.

You say you're overspending on toys? Those snot-nosed kids are gonna break them in a week anyway. There is no Santa Claus. So tell them! Tell them you're tired of lying about some weird bearded Teletubby who hangs with elves and breaks into people's houses through chimneys.

Trying to make up for treating your wife like crap all year by buying her some cheap bauble? Forget it. She doesn't want that mass-produced knockoff brown-diamond tennis bracelet. She's gonna return it the day after Christmas and get back the 99 bucks anyway.

So do yourself a favor. Have a nice romantic Christmas dinner and use what you didn't spend to do what you should have been doing all along.

Buy me a birthday gift!

Me and all the December babies you know.

I'm calling on all my December people to join the movement. Because the fact of the matter is, you owe us.

You owe us for every time you faked the birthday funk. For every Pollyanna gift you recycled. For every fruitcake that cracked our teeth.

You owe us.

Holla if you hear me, December babies! We are taking back our birthday heritage!

This revolution will not be televised, so don't look for me on any of those diamond commercials with the classical violins and rich folks in silhouette.

I'm not looking to open the bathroom cabinet and have the keys to a Lexus drop in my lap.

This is a grassroots movement to bring birthday cards and gifts to every December baby, no matter their race, creed or ethnicity. Leave no Sagittarius or Capricorn behind!

You think I'm crazy? Maybe I am. But you can't judge me any more than you can judge the rest of my December brethren. We've spent years holding back our discontent, smiling and saying "thank you" when we really mean, "Where's the rest of my loot?"

So here's the deal. We want two gifts--one on our birthday, and one on Christmas. Starting this year.

And for your convenience, here's a list of items we will not accept:

- Toilet paper with knitted covering. (Don't laugh. I've seen it.)
- Chia Pets. (This includes the *Scooby-Doo* variety.)
- Fruitcakes. (Cool if y'all could cook, but most of you can't.)
- Fancy soaps. (No matter how you slice it, you're saying we stink.)
- E-cards. (Flash technology aside, these are free, and therefore unacceptable.)

You'd be wise to cooperate. December people are everywhere. And we're not afraid to mobilize.

We've got grandmothers in Iowa and ballers in

North Philly, Russians in Chicago and Ethiopians in Atlanta, Cambodians in New York and Italians in New Jersey.

From London, England to Los Angeles, California, from the Virgin Islands to Honolulu, Hawaii, we are everyone, we are everywhere, and we are speaking with one voice.

In fact, now that I think about it, not only do we want two gifts this December, we want makeup gifts for all the years we got the shaft.

Now that I think about it ... we want makeup gifts for all the years we got the shaft.

Using myself as an example, here's how it's going to work:

I'm turning 35 this year. The two-gift December bonanza ended when I was about 10. Simply put, I'm owed an extra gift from everyone I've known for each of the last 25 years.

I'm not trying to break anybody, so let's say each gift is valued at about $20. I don't have many friends, and I've got a small family, so let's make it an even 10 gifts per year. Ten gifts at $20 each, over 25 years. That comes out to about $5,000.

I'll take my birthday reparations in cash, please. In fact, let me speak for my December baby brethren: We'll all take it in cash.

So if you don't want a multicultural, multiethnic, pissed-off hoard of December babies crashing your holiday party this year, I suggest you whip out your checkbooks this minute and get started.

The name is Jones. It's not hard to spell.

Coming Out

At last, I'm revealing the belly I've been hiding from the world.

Every day when I get home, my 15-month-old daughter plays a game called Bellysmack. It goes a little something like this.

I walk in the door. Eve yells, "Dada!" and jumps into my arms. We laugh. I put her down. She runs across the living room and waits for me to remove my sweater or jacket or whatever I happen to be wearing over my T-shirt.

Once I'm on the couch, she stands in front of me until I lift her onto my lap. Then she sticks her thumb contentedly into her mouth, smiles and pulls at my T-shirt with all her might.

The object of Bellysmack is simple. Eve's goal is to reveal the belly I've been hiding from the world. Once exposed, she smacks it as many times as she can before the shame of watching my own fat jiggle forces me to tuck my T-shirt back in.

Bellysmack came into being because at the tender age of 35, I have developed a stomach that consists of huddled masses of fat yearning to be free. It's a stomach, quite frankly, that has taken on a life of its own. It's so bad, I'm waiting for my stomach to jump up and pull a stunt like that plant in *Little Shop of Horrors*.

"Feed me, Solomon!"

"No, I can't do it anymore. It's not right. Hey, what are you--"

"Buuurrraaahhh!!!"

Just like that. Eaten by my own stomach.

I don't want it to come to that. So before my stomach takes on Buddhalike proportions, before sumo wrestlers begin challenging me on the street, before I get an invitation to some inane celebration of gluttony like

Philadelphia's *Wing Bowl*, I'm going to take action.

That's right, Solomon's going on a diet.

Don't get me wrong. It's not like I'm Sherman Klump. Years of push-ups have given me a fairly muscular chest and solid arms. Lots of walking has made my legs pretty strong, too.

But my stomach ...

Wait, if I'm going to accept this, I have to recognize it for what it is. I don't have a stomach. I have a gut. An out-of-control gut.

I don't have a beer belly. My belly's grown to its current level of rotundity without the benefit of Budweiser or Coors, Olde English or Colt 45. It has, in fact, achieved blissful roundness with the help of only relatively few foodstuffs, habits and people.

And so, before I set about getting rid of my stomach, I'd like to thank everyone who helped make this moment of clarity possible.

First on the list--me. I'm insatiable. Next is my mom. Her sweet potato pies will make you slap your grandmother. I'd also like to thank my wife, LaVeta. She makes maple butter pecan ice cream from scratch.

The list is rounded out by the usual suspects: McDonald's, whose dollar menu makes gluttony way too convenient; Wendy's, whose No. 1 with cheese and a Frosty is a near-sexual hamburger experience; and Crown Fried Chicken, whose $3.99 lunch special with hot sauce packets gives me goosebumps.

I ain't even gonna mention Lee's Hoagies or Pat's King of Steaks.

When LaVeta and I started dating, I was weightlifting and swimming. But even then, at my semibuffed best, my stomach was beginning to creep over the top of my pants.

I pretended not to notice. Then one day as we were finishing up one of my mother's succulent calorie-laden dinners, LaVeta noticed.

As her eyes lingered at my stomach, I went into smooth-talk mode. "Oh, don't worry about that, Baby," I told her. "It goes down after I digest my food."

I was lying. But I didn't know it. I'd told myself that same lie so many times that I'd come to believe it.

Now, six years later, I can't lie to myself anymore. Even though most mornings I do 96 push-ups and 100 crunches--which have the sole effect of making my fat stomach harder--not much has changed.

In fact, my gut is getting worse.

So before I allow Eve to play Bellysmack again, before I begin wearing my pants over my navel to hide my growing belly, before LaVeta makes another wisecrack about my being pregnant, I'm going to make some changes.

Starting today, starting right now, I'm going to commit to eating one Wendy's hamburger per week (instead of two), a monthly cup of maple butter pecan ice cream (instead of a pint) and one slice of sweet potato pie per Christmas (instead of four).

Wow. I feel healthier already. I'm glad I made those commitments.

Now pass me a Baby Ruth. I ain't say nothin' about no candy.

Calling All Bag Ladies

I've got what you want. Wrapped in stained brown paper.

Rotisserie vermin and squirming earthworms are best consumed in private. That's why I usually don't watch reality shows. They make me feel like I'm intruding on a personal moment.

But when I saw the advertisements for *Joe Millionaire*, my attitude changed. I wanted to see the gold diggers exposed, humiliated, destroyed.

Then Zora, the Jersey girl, won the heart of Evan, the fake multimillionaire. When she agreed to date him in spite of his uncanny ability to manipulate 20 women at once, the lack of Springerlike fireworks was extremely disappointing.

That's why I've decided, at my wife's urging, to create my own reality dating show.

Here's the premise: A guy is dropped onto a college campus with a sandwich, potato chips and a soda. He's given hundreds of hungry coeds to choose from, and eliminates them based on imperfections ranging from cottage cheese thighs to hair weaves that resemble sun-baked hay.

Anyway, the guy's broke, and the women know it. But he's got food, and the women want it. They are, after all, in college. Which means they're broke, too.

If the women can highlight their strengths, hide their deficiencies and destroy the competition, they get the chance to capture the coveted prize: half a sandwich. I've named my reality show *Joe Lunchbag*.

I know I can make this concept work, because when my wife and I met in college, I was Joe Lunchbag. I had no money, no real job and no car. But I invariably squirreled away enough money to buy a bacon, egg and cheese sandwich before my morning classes at Temple. And in the afternoon I usually managed a turkey and cheese sandwich, a bag of Lay's and a Hawaiian Punch.

"You always had food," LaVeta later admitted to me. It was the kind of confession you might hear on *Joe Lunchbag: The Aftermath*. "And it was always in a brown paper bag with a grease stain on it."

Indeed, she wasn't the only one who noticed.

I showed one chick my lunch bag, and she started picking me up in a Lexus at my mama's house. Another used to call me day and night--on my mama's phone. Still another took me to one of those poetry cafes where people drink espresso and do spoken-word readings.

The lunch bags had elevated me. I wasn't just some broke dude living in his mama's house anymore. I was a meal ticket.

Perhaps that's why LaVeta bumped into me as I returned from a campus sandwich vendor with a bag in my hand.

As I talked to her, I could feel that there was something different about me. The lunch bag had made me suave, debonair, cool. She gave me her number. And after that, I decided to eliminate some of the other contestants from the show.

First I banished the caller. She talked too much. Next I ditched the poetry chick. Too hip for me. Then I got rid of Ms. Lexus. She was ... how shall we say ... sanity challenged.

By the time I narrowed down the field to several possible winners, LaVeta had decided she was going to get that sandwich, whatever the cost.

She began by looking at my lunch bags and dropping hints like, "Boy, I sure am hungry."

Like *Joe Millionaire* with Zora, LaVeta's seeming innocence left me utterly defenseless. I had to ask her out. When I did, and she answered the door looking like a cross between Tyra Banks and Beyoncé Knowles, I was smitten.

I sent flowers to her classes. I walked her home from the subway. And eventually, before we even kissed, I did the unthinkable.

I shared a sandwich with her.

Six years later, the days of *Joe Lunchbag* are long gone. LaVeta and I are married. Our daughter, Eve, is running around the house. And the freedom to eat a sandwich in peace has just about vanished.

But I still think I can do a reality show. I've got plenty of ideas. And I've experienced each one of them. When Eve was born, and I revisited the realities of childbirth, I was almost *Joe Barf Bag*. On Tuesdays, our trash day, I invariably become *Joe Garbage Bag*. On Sunday, when we take the baby to church, I'm *Joe Diaper Bag*.

And when I change the liner in the Diaper Champ--the little doohickey that's supposed to contain the smell of used diapers--I become my personal favorite, *Joe Doo Doo Bag*.

Think women would compete for a guy like that?

Stay tuned. *Joe Lunchbag* may hit the airwaves this fall.

Sixers announce new coach: Solomon Jones

Y'all want a guy who'll win some rings.
Try me!

I'm not a huge Sixers fan. Haven't been since the day they got rid of Mo Cheeks, the point guard from the '83 championship team. It wasn't so much that they decided to let him go, but the fact that he found out about being traded from a reporter. Seems then-owner Harold Katz conveniently forgot to tell him.

Ironic, isn't it? Every wannabe sports aficionado in Philadelphia has just spent months trying to pencil in the very same Maurice Cheeks as the replacement for the stream of coaches who've left in the past year.

Well, by now everyone's got the news flash--Mo ain't comin' back.

So instead of pining for the days of yesteryear, y'all need to start thinkin' outside the box.

You want a coach with a fresh approach? A guy who's not afraid to experiment? A guy who'll win some rings?

How does this sound--Coach Solomon Jones?

I'm putting the basketball world on notice. I want to coach the Philadelphia 76ers. And if I don't get a call from team president Billy King in the next day or so, I'm going straight to the man in charge.

Not 76ers team owner Ed Snider. Uh uh. I'm gonna wait till 'bout 2 a.m. Friday or Saturday night, march right down to one of those clubs 'round Second and Market, push my way past the velvet rope leading to the VIP section and take my case straight to the Man. Allen Iverson.

I'll make one promise: to get one more guy like

him. A player who will fearlessly take on the opposition and score a gazillion points, fueled by nothing more than KFC, Baby Ruths and Taco Bell.

No weightlifting. No rules.

Most of all, I'll make this point very clear: Starting with the Coach Solomon Jones regime, no practice.

Okay, so I know virtually nothing about basketball. I was the last guy picked when I played in an intramural basketball league in junior high, which is hard to do in an academic school with no real jocks.

I also have no real experience as a coach at any level, unless you count the time I instructed my wife LaVeta to push when she was having our daughter, Eve.

But if you give me $6 million a year, like they gave Larry Brown, I'll go door-to-door selling dirty drawers. Have you buyin' 'em, too!

Which brings me to my point. The way I figure it, motivating multimillionaires who've spent most of their young adult lives being coddled by society can't be that much harder than selling dirty Fruit of the Looms. All you have to do is apply yourself.

I'll take my cues from departed coach Larry Brown.

When the team gets way behind, I'll sit there, chin in hand, then jump up and yell crazy stuff at the referee.

If my guy takes a hard foul, for example, I'll run up to the ref and scream, "There are no weapons of mass destruction in Iraq!"

While the ref tries to figure out whether to call a technical foul or the police, I'll lunge at him while my players pull me back to the bench.

"You lucky they holdin' me, ref! You reeeeaaaal lucky!"

When one of my players doesn't get a call, I'll run up to the ref again. "I hate raspberry sherbet! In fact,

I hate all sherbet! Men shouldn't eat sherbet! It's chick food!"

When the ref ejects me from the game, chants of "Win one for Baldy" will begin at the far end of the Wachovia Center, then spread like wildfire throughout the building. Inspired by the support for Coach Solomon Jones, the Sixers will go on a run and win.

Come the postgame press conference, I'll talk in monotones.

"The little kid did a great job tonight. That last shot, the game winner, was just how we drew it up in practice. I can't say enough about the little kid."

See, y'all wouldn't have to know we didn't have practice. I mean, how much practice does it take to teach everybody to stand around while Allen does all the work?

Finally, I should be the coach of the Sixers because Billy King and I would be the two smoothest bald black dudes with goatees in the NBA.

We'd be poster children for chocolate baldness, sitting next to each other at press conferences looking like two well-paid Milk Duds.

In fact, that would be our first marketing campaign. We'd give out little Milk Dud bobblehead dolls with goatees.

Billy's would have glasses. Mine would be smiling--a Milk Dud with teeth.

Scoff not. The reality is, there's only one sure route to a Sixers championship. Me. Coach Solomon Jones.

No practice, no training, no weight rooms. The players can do what they want and eat what they want--including a generous helping of Milk Duds, the new officially endorsed Philadelphia 76ers team snack.

Tell you what. I'll make y'all forget about Maurice Cheeks real quick.

Tool Envy

I'm man enough to admit my equipment comes up short.

For those who need an update on the travails of the Joneses, we've spent the past few weeks painting our new home, and in the process, discovering that the boogieman once lived there.

Finding nasal matter on the walls was a shocking, stomach-churning turn of events. But we persevered, scraped the boogies from the otherwise pristine walls, then had the carpets cleaned by a professional (because who knows what the boogieman may have done to the rugs?).

When we were sure we'd scrubbed away the last vestiges of the previous regime, we moved in a week and a half ago.

But as we unpacked boxes, appliances, window treatments and furniture, I discovered that I had bigger problems than moving in behind a chronic nosepicker.

Eve's crib needed to be put back together. The dining room set had to be reconstructed. The washer and dryer had to be set up. Curtains needed to be hung. Stuff had to be fixed.

Of course the fact that I'm about as handy as my 2-year-old was a problem. But there was more to it than my lack of handyman acumen.

The fact of the matter is I couldn't fix and construct all that stuff, even if I wanted to. Because I've got only one tool.

I got my Ryobi 9.6-volt electric screwdriver when we were living in our last place, because I was tired of trying to screw curtain rods into rock-hard woodwork with sweaty hands, a 10-year-old Phillips head screwdriver and a bad attitude.

Not that the manual labor was a bad thing. It made my fingers really muscular, which is cool if you want to be governor of California and you need the extra hand strength to grope women. But hey, I'm a writer, and I need my fingers to be nimble. So I made the investment in the Ryobi. And what an investment it was.

That's when the reality hit me. I don't know how to fix nothin'...

The thing can drive screws or remove them. It has two bits, for Phillips head or regular screws, big or small. And it runs on a rechargeable battery, which is good for me, because if it had a cord, I'd trip over it. While on a ladder. Guaranteed.

But anyway, it's a cool tool. So cool that when I got it, I started to think I was a baller--the Big Willie of tool owners. I pictured myself up on a ladder, my electric screwdriver hanging from a leather tool belt, as the theme from *The Good, the Bad and the Ugly* played tantalizingly in the background.

I saw myself installing a roof, repairing an electrical system, building a house. All with my electric screwdriver.

But then we moved into our own home, and all our stuff was sitting there, waiting to be put back together after months in storage. That's when the reality hit me. I don't know how to fix nothin', never did know how to fix nothin' and probably never will know how to fix nothin'.

That's when we had to call in the big guns--the man whose tool collection makes my electric screwdriver look like a peashooter.

That's right, ladies and gentlemen. We had to call my father-in-law.

This is a guy who used to design and build furniture, refurbished several houses and once built a house from the ground up.

Without revealing too much, let's just say this. The man don't have a tool box. He's got a tool shed. We lovingly call it the Home Depot Annex.

He's got a tool for every occasion. He helped us through the boogie crisis by lending us a screwdriver that we used not only to screw in outlet covers, but also to scrape off boogies. (He was kind enough to let us keep it when he learned what it had been used for.)

He's got drills. He's got hammers. He even has a set of those hex things that mere mortals have seen only with Ikea furniture. And thank God. Because without him, there's no way I would've been able to reconstruct our dining room table, Eve's crib, our refrigerator or our bed.

Of course watching him do his magic (he wouldn't let me help him, correctly assuming I'd only get in the way) has left me with tool envy.

And it's left me rethinking my dependence on a single electric screwdriver. As a homeowner, I think I might actually have to invest in a toolbox someday.

Until then, I'll be making frequent visits to the Home Depot Annex. And hoping that my father-in-law will continue to keep me out of the way.

Fat Free At Last

One man's quest to avoid death by cheesesteak.

Remember when I admitted that my slight paunch had gone out of control, prompting my daughter Eve to invent a game called Bellysmack? Remember I said that her fascination with my stomach had prompted me to go on a diet?

Well, I lied. Not intentionally, of course. It was just one of those things.

One day I was eating salads and drinking water. A few days later I was right back at Crown Fried Chicken, eating a three-piece and an order of fries, while clutching those heavenly hot sauce packets I can't seem to live without.

In one fell swoop, I went from watercress to Wendy's, from iceberg lettuce to ice cream sandwiches. I fell hard upon the slippery slope of caloric intake, until finally, in an orgy of gluttony, I set out with reckless abandon to find my food of choice.

That's right. I stood in line at Pat's King of Steaks and ordered a heart attack with onions.

"Don't worry," said the lady behind the counter, as I forked over a 20 to pay for a steak sandwich slathered with Cheez Whiz, provolone and American. "You don't actually have the heart attack for about 20 years."

For normal people, that would've been right. But I'm a man whose idea of dieting--and you'll recall this from the Bellysmack column--is one Snickers instead of two, one trip to McDonald's instead of three, and a two-piece instead of a meal.

I'm afraid, dear readers, that my gluttony has finally caught up with me. The results of my last physical are in. My date with the heart attack is imminent. My cholesterol is off the charts.

I don't know if my doctor actually knew that my blood test results would come back with enough cholesterol to kill a large mammal. But I do know that he counseled me about a living will during my physical, and even gave me the paperwork necessary to execute one.

He said he gives that paper to all his patients. But I think he smelled the fried chicken on my clothes. And he gave me the paper in case I passed out while in the middle of eating a heart attack--or worse, having one.

Further, I believe he looked over my blood test results, and before taking out the standard form and checking "abnormal" in the cholesterol column, he called up Johns Hopkins and proposed making me into a cholesterol experiment.

"Doctor? Got a case study for you. Thirty-five-year-old African- American male, no history of heart disease, with the odor of cheese-steaks and fried chicken embedded in his clothing. Cholesterol level is the highest I've ever seen. If we can get this guy back to normal, we could be published in The *New England Journal of Medicine*. We could change the lives of millions. We could win the Nobel Prize!"

A long pause on the phone.

"Sounds like an interesting case study," says the Johns Hopkins guy. "I've just got one question."

"Yes?"

"Does he have any more of that chicken? I'm kinda hungry."

Okay, maybe he didn't call Johns Hopkins. But I don't care. I'm gonna lick this thing. Without Lipitor, without therapy and without any of that other cholesterol-lowering crap they try to push on you these days.

I'm gonna do it the old-fashioned way. I'm gonna show some discipline, change my diet and indulge my daughter Eve in her newest game--riding Daddy's back while he does all manner of torturous exercises.

Sure, I'm gonna miss my heart-attack cheesesteaks, my McDonald's french fries and my Wendy's singles. And when I think of Crown Fried Chicken, I'll just have to go into one of my drawers at work and clutch one of those little hot sauce packets that I love so much (and yes, I do keep them in my drawer).

Maybe, just maybe, I can also stop stressing about life's little ups and downs, such as the fact that I'm now out of vices. Gave up mood-altering substances seven years ago, along with alcohol, cigarettes, running the streets and running women.

Got married a few years ago, settled down and officially became a homebody. Now they're taking away the one indulgence I had left. To which I can only say one thing:

Goodbye, cholesterol-laden foodstuffs. I'll miss you. I'll really, really miss you.

Bring the funk

True confessions of a novelist in need of a shower.

I recently took a week off from my day job to put the finishing touches on my new novel, *Ride or Die*. To understand the significance of that, you have to understand the true nature of writers.

We are grubby little creatures who labor in darkness, away from the lure of real food, showers and the light of day. In our best moments at work, we are you--when you wouldn't dare get close to another human being.

When I wrote my last book, I stayed at home for a month, and in the process, I lost about 10 pounds. When I came back to work, people asked me if I was okay.

There were conspiratorial whispers.

"Do you think he's ... ill ?"

Raised eyebrows.

"You know he's had that *drug* thing ... "

Fact of the matter was, I was doing what writers do--banging out 90,000 words while under the influence of stale coffee and sleeplessness.

It's hard to do that these days. Because now I've got a family.

These last few months my writing has routinely kept me up until at least 1 o'clock in the morning. And during this time, I've realized a few things about myself. LaVeta has, too.

One recent morning, when I got into bed after a particularly long writing session, she turned to me with her nose scrunched up and asked the question that all writers must eventually face.

"Is that your underarms?"

Without even sniffing to confirm, I knew it was. Overnight, the Sure I was using had morphed into Uncertain, and then to Definitely Not.

You see, deodorant is designed for people who toil through a regular workday. It's not for guys like me, who work an eight-hour job, come home and strap themselves to computers to work for another eight hours.

Out of love for my wife, I now wash up after writing.

Of course the funk doesn't matter to Eve.

"Pay, Daddy!" she said, marching into our little home office and crawling onto my lap a couple weeks ago.

She was trying to say "play," but "pay" was the more appropriate term. Because at that moment, while I was sitting there trying to finish my latest book, little Eve was intent on giving me a dose of reality.

She began to fiddle with the keyboard, pressing buttons in strange combinations. When she pressed a button and I thought I heard the voice of Darth Vader emerge from the speakers, I had to make her get down. This was met with screams of bloody murder.

In an attempt to keep the kid quiet, I relented. And before it was all over, she had me on the floor doing pushups.

When LaVeta came upstairs, Eve bragged about her victory.

"Mommy, look!"

LaVeta did. And there I was, a defeated beast of burden, sweating out pushup No. 20, while a 30-pound Marine Corps drill instructor rode on my back, laughing.

If I was to have any hope of ever finishing the book, I'd have to leave my house in the dead of winter, with nothing but the clothes on my back, and not take a backward glance.

I did, and when I arrived at my mother's place

without a toothbrush or a change of clothes, I knew I was in writer mode--stinky underarms and all.

I stayed there the first night, in my mother's little office, and typed until I couldn't think anymore. Then I slept in my clothes, awoke the next day and continued, while imbibing big cups of coffee.

I did this a few more times, going home now and then to bathe, and coming back without shaving. By the fourth day I looked like hell. And like a Lamborghini shifting effortlessly into fourth gear, my mother went into caretaker mode.

A plate of fattening food I shouldn't have been eating miraculously appeared on the table, along with buttered bread and a tall glass of juice.

She went to the store to buy toiletries (okay, I asked her to pick me up a few things, but just go with it). She even made me stop writing at one point and forced me to eat a plate of baked chicken.

But it was all good, because the family pulled together to see me through.

LaVeta read through a draft of the nearly completed book for me and brought the corrections to my mother's house. Eve called on my cell phone at critical points with the brilliant and uplifting words, "Hi Daddy!" And my mom continued to make me eat, even when I didn't want to.

And so, when my new book hits the shelves this summer, remember that I didn't do it alone. Then run out to the bookstores clutching $20 bills, and try not to think about the funk.

Sesame Seeds

Educational TV is helping my daughter . . . but it's killing me.

Our 2-year-old daughter Eve spends a lot of time watching television. We spend a lot of time trying to get her to stop. It's not because we're against television. We just hate listening to the high-pitched voices of *Sesame Street* characters cascading through our living room.

But our preferences don't really matter when it comes to *Sesame Street*. Because Eve, like most toddlers, can watch it for days, weeks, even months at a time. All she needs is a bowl of cheese curls, a cup of grape juice and a little space--in case she gets the sudden urge to participate in some *Sesame Street*-inspired production number.

Until now we didn't see the harm in letting her engage her *Sesame Street* obsession. I mean, she's already memorized the alphabet with the help of the Big Bird alphabet support group.

But a study that was published in the April issue of *Pediatrics* has us rethinking our permissive attitude toward all that educational TV watchin'.

Apparently, by allowing Eve to watch so much *Sesame Street*, we may be increasing her risk of developing attention deficit/hyperactivity disorder (ADHD), which the study tells us affects between 4 and 12 percent of American children, making it the most common behavioral disorder of childhood.

Boy, do I feel stupid. I was under the impression that America's misbehaving, disrespectful kids just needed attention from their parents and an occasional whack on the bottom.

Thanks to the study, I realize that America's TV addicted kids really do need help. And maybe our adults do too.

I used to think that my inability to concentrate was because I was just naturally high strung. But now I'm convinced that it's the result of all those *Schoolhouse Rock-, Electric Company-* and *Sesame Street*-related thoughts going through my head.

For instance, when I see my daughter watching *Sesame Street*, I can't hear the alphabet songs because I'm too busy wondering how Maria can still look exactly the same way she did when I was, like, 7.

Sometimes those *Schoolhouse Rock* songs pop into my head too. Truth be told, I'm struggling against the urge to break into the *Schoolhouse Rock* constitutional preamble song at this very moment. Can't ... hold ... out ... much ... longer!

"We the people, in order to form a more perfect union, establish justice, ensure domestic tranquility, provide for the common defense, promote the general welfare, and secure the blessings of liberty to ourselves and our posterity, do ordain and establish this Constitution for the United States of America ... United States of America."

Oh no! Here comes another one. Stand back!

"I'm just a bill, yes, I'm only a bill, and I'm sitting here on Capitol Hill. Well, it's a long, long journey to the capital city. It's a long, long wait while I'm sitting in committee. But I know I'll be a law someday ... At least I hope and pray that I will, but today I'm still just a bill."

Okay. I'm fine now. Just had an ADHD moment. It's sort of like the moments I have when I see Morgan Freeman in a movie and remember that he got his start playing Easy Reader in the *Children's Television Workshop* show *The Electric Company.*

Or like the ADHD moments I have when I see trains hooking up, and suddenly start singing the *Schoolhouse Rock* conjunction song.

"Conjunction junction, what's your function?

Hooking up words and phrases and clauses. Conjunction junction, how's that function? I got three favorite cars that get most of my job done. Conjunction junction, what's their function? I got "and," "but" and "or." They'll get you pretty far."

I guess watching all that TV as a kid really has warped my mind. I can't stop thinking about the preamble to the Constitution, or the legislative process that allows a bill to become law, or the fact that conjunctions are the linking words that connect phrases.

Who would've thought that the songs I heard on television as a toddler would still be in my head at the ripe old age of 36? Who would've thought that those little songs would prevent me from concentrating on the important things in life? I mean, who needs to know anything about the Constitution?

Maybe I should try to fight this thing while I have the chance. Maybe I should start taking Ritalin. Maybe I should try to get de-programmed or something.

Or maybe, just maybe, I should sit down next to Eve and take in a couple episodes of *Sesame Street.* I might not get rid of my ADHD. But I might just learn something.

It Runs In The Family

At last there's proof. No one can keep up with a Jones.

Kentucky Derby and Preakness Stakes winner Smarty Jones was raised and trained in Philadelphia Park, which means he's technically from the 'hood. And like everyone else in Philadelphia, I like winners from the 'hood.

You see, we Philadelphians are desperate to connect ourselves to winners. Need examples?

Well, Rocky Balboa didn't even exist. But I went to school with a dude who swore Rocky was his uncle.

Will Smith? Back when I was a rapper, he was just some dude from West Philly I shared the stage with. Neither of us was a superstar. But now that he's making $20 million a film, he's got women all over the city vying for the right to be his baby's mama. (I know he's married, but that's just a technicality to a hoochie.)

The point is, we Philadelphians are willing to go to any lengths to be associated with success. Don't believe me? I know a dude named Bop from 25th and Jefferson who has the deep black complexion of Sidney Poitier, yet he swears that Robert De Niro is his daddy. When you ask him how that could be, he's indignant.

"You know he got jungle fever!" Bop says. "Didn't you see him with Angela Bassett?"

"Yeah, Bop. But Angela's not your mom, and Robert De Niro's never been down here to see you."

"He busy, man! Stop hatin'!"

And so it goes.

Given our sordid history of lying to associate ourselves with celebrities, I know that what I'm about to say will be met with skepticism. But I have to say it nonetheless. I didn't watch the Kentucky Derby merely as an interested Philadelphian.

I watched because Smarty Jones is my cousin.

I know what you're thinking. You're thinking, "Smarty Jones is a horse. There's no way Solomon can be related to him." But the evidence of our relationship is clear. He's smart. I'm smart. His name is Jones. My name is Jones.

Need more proof? Well, Smarty Jones once reared up and hit his head on a piece of unpadded iron on a starting gate at Philadelphia Park. He cracked his skull. Rumor has it you can still see the dent in his head.

It just so happens that I also hit my head once. I did it while coming down the steps in my house. It really hurt. And if you look at the top of my head very closely, you can still see the dent.

But the similarities don't end there. Smarty Jones can run extremely fast with a jockey on his back. And though I don't claim to be able to carry a 125-pound man for a mile and a quarter, I do a mean piggyback while carrying my 2-year-old daughter, Eve. My wife once clocked me at about 1 mile per hour.

The way I figure it, that's the equivalent of winning the Kentucky Derby.

I see that look on your face. You're still skeptical. You're thinking, "Even with all these similarities--the name, the intellect, the speed, the head dents--there's no way Solomon and Smarty can be blood relatives. Humans and horses aren't compatible."

Well, we wouldn't be under normal circumstances. But the way our families came together was far from normal.

It was the late '50s, at the height of the Cold War, and the government was desperate to find the perfect spy. Inspired by the classic movie *The Fly*, the government (we're still not sure which agency) came up with a great plan. They would send a super-intelligent horse into the

Soviet Union to spy on the Kremlin.

My great-great-uncle Ed was a genius and a decorated war hero. He volunteered to allow his intelligence to be transferred to a horse. But when government scientists put my uncle in one pod and a horse in the other, something went terribly wrong. My uncle was horribly disfigured, and took on the shape of a horse. The only thing left intact was his voice.

After years of counseling and treatment, my uncle went on with his life. He found love with a mare that understood him. He even became a television star. Perhaps you've heard of him. They called him Mister Ed. But to us, he was just Uncle Ed. Uncle Ed Jones.

Uncle Ed and his wife had many children. One of them was Smarty Jones' great-great-grandmom, Farty Jones. And now, a couple generations later, my uncle's legacy lives on in Smarty.

I'm proud of my cousin Smarty. He's done well for himself. That's why I'm only going to ask for a few hundred thousand of his winnings. After all, we Joneses got to stick together.

Boobs

Community Chest

The boobs are out again. It's our job to restrain them.

As I've gotten older, I've discovered that spring holds much promise. But that ain't necessarily a good thing.

With spring comes allergies, which I seem to have contracted along with the excess fat, bloated credit card bills and head-of-state-like responsibilities that come with a wife and kids.

Spring hosts the annual con game that turns a religious celebration into a mishmash of bunnies, chocolate candy, painted eggs and commercialism. And of course, we can't forget that giant sucking sound we hear every April 15: taxes.

But that's not the worst of it. What's most intolerable about spring is people. Not all people, you understand. Just certain people.

You know the ones. They come in different shapes, sizes and colors, and bounce around without a care in the world. They often have to be restrained. And though they frequently travel in pairs, they occasionally pop out one at a time (*see Jackson, Janet*).

They're boobs. And we're surrounded by them. Especially in spring.

The little boobs (let's call them B cups) are the ones who feel like springtime is the perfect time to start jogging, Rollerblading or bike-riding.

These are most often professional boobs--investment bankers, lawyers and the like. Boobs of some means. Boobs who feel that they can run 10 miles at the drop of a hat.

Of course there's nothing wrong with a little spring exercise, if you've actually engaged in some semblance of physical activity during winter. Sadly, most boobs have not. And when they take to the road in the spring, they're dangerous.

No doubt you've seen these boobs bouncing along jogging paths this spring. They're the ones who have the latest workout gear, the state-of-the-art safety equipment and absolutely no idea what they're doing.

If you're watching one of them Rollerblade right now, they will trip and fall at least three times in the next 60 seconds, then wander into the street, where a speeding SUV of tank-like proportions will barely miss them.

If you're wondering why these boobs are never hurt in such incidents, you don't understand the main rule of boobdom.

That is, no matter how stupid the boob's activity, the boob is never the one to get injured.

Because boobs have a tremendous capacity for bouncing back.

Medium boobs (for consistency's sake, let's call them C cups) are a little more annoying. These are the people who feel that spring is the perfect time to debut their gazillion-dollar car stereo system.

It's got a 30-disc CD changer, two subwoofers, a billion-watt amplifier, 24-track equalizer, 15 speakers, and only works between the hours of midnight and 4 a.m. ... on weeknights.

Now if you're one of the boobs who fit this category, please understand that I'm not against car stereos. I like music, too. But if your stereo costs more than your car, you're a boob. If, whenever you turn on the stereo, the bolts holding together your 15-year-old Hyundai begin to loosen, you're a boob. If you've taken out your backseat because it's more important to have DMX in your car than it is to have your kid in it, guess what? You're a boob.

And if you ride by my house bangin' Eminem at 3 o'clock in the morning when I have to get up and go to work the next day, you're a boob. An obviously unemployed boob.

That's the problem with boobs. They spend way too much time just hangin' around.

Which brings me to the big boobs. That's right. The D cups. These are the people who use spring to engage in kamikaze missions that could result in serious injury to someone--most likely not them.

You've got boobs on four-wheel off-road vehicles, riding the wrong way on major city thoroughfares. No helmet. No pads. No license. No problem.

You've got suburban boobs who steal shopping carts and reenact stunts from the movie *Jackass* (which, by the way, is another name for boob).

You've even got boobs who'll try to convince you that boobism is okay. That you should accept boob-like behavior in the name of diversity. That boobs should be allowed to live openly.

Well, I say no!

Because the fact of the matter is, we've got enough to deal with during springtime. We don't need to see boobs, too.

The Long and Short of It

Don't overdo the do. Bald is beautiful, too

I like long hair as much as the next guy. Really, I do. The fact of the matter is, my wife's luxurious mane was one of the first things I noticed about her.

That's not to say that ladies with short hair are unattractive. They look good too. Just depends on where the hair is. If the hair is under their arms--lookin' like they've got Buckwheat in a headlock, or somethin'--that ain't cool. If they've got carpeting on their backs, pony-tails in their ears or AstroTurf on their legs, well, that ain't cool either.

But a woman who has short hair on her head can be as fine as the next woman. That's why I don't under-stand women who go overboard in their attempts to obtain long hair. Because the fact of the matter is, there are times when long hair ain't lovely.

At what times, you ask? Well, the times vary, but the methods are always the same. And because I want women to look their best, I am going to address this con-troversy head-on.

That's right, I'm talking wigs, weaves and worms.

Time was, women who wore wigs set limits for them-selves. The wig had to be somewhere close to the woman's natural hair color. It had to be tasteful in its appearance. It had to be a reasonable length.

No more.

Since the advent of the music video, young women have taken to engaging in all-day open auditions for MTV clown of the week.

Because of this development, I regret to have to step in and set boundaries for my wig-wearing sisters.

They are as follows:

If the wig's hair has the consistency of wire, the strength of a bulletproof vest and sits atop your head like a bird's nest, you are not wearing a wig. You're wearing a helmet. If you have not received orders to the Persian Gulf in recent days, remove it immediately. It's an insult to our troops.

If the edges of your wig are lint-lined and curling away from your scalp, the wig is afraid. It's trying--in the only way an inanimate object can--to run away. Chances are, you haven't washed your *real* hair lately, and the wig is afraid to actually touch you. Remove the wig immediately, proceed to the nearest shower ... and take one.

Finally, if your wig smells like a game of three-on-three, refer to the prior paragraph, and follow the same procedure.

Unfortunately, weaves are even more problematic than

wigs. This is because the weave, by its very nature, is an overt attempt to deceive.

How else do you explain trying to make people believe that your hair, which was 2 inches long and curly on Wednesday, is 18 inches long and straight on Friday? Ain't that much Rogaine in the world.

That's why we have to have guidelines. Follow them, and you, too, can successfully wear a weave.

First, monitor the length. If, when your hairdresser is finished sewing and gluing, you emerge from the salon looking like Cousin Itt, you have too much weave. When you finish tripping over your ankle-length monstrosity, return to the beautician's chair and have it cut to shoulder-length.

Second, monitor the texture. And this is sensitive, because some people have come to believe that there is good and bad hair. Well, I'm here to tell you that the only bad hair is bought hair. If God gave you peasy, don't make it cheesy. Stick with what you got. You've got more options with yours than those straight-haired chicks, anyway.

But getting back to the weaves. If your hair is kinky and brown, don't buy hair that's straight and black. You look (how can I say this tactfully?) stupid.

Finally, we have to address the worm thing. This is not about wigs or weaves. It's about both.

If your wig or weave looks like Oodles of Noodles, spaghetti or yarn, it fits into this category. If this is the case, be considerate. Carry a fork when you walk down the street. Somebody might want to sample your 'do.

If you can't at least do that much, you might want to consider the Solomon Jones look.

Take it off. Take it all off.

Duck and Cover

Don't die of exposure. Follow my warm weather survival guide.

You've heard Nelly's hit single "Hot in Herre." It's on the radio. It's on award shows. It's even in the Chris Rock movie, *Head of State*, which features old white folks in formalwear dancing to rap music--a concept I'm convinced was stolen from one of my stories.

But I digress. The song, and this story, is about people taking their clothes off when it's hot. While Nelly encourages it, I don't. Because most people shouldn't publicly disrobe. They really shouldn't.

In fact, when Nelly says "It's gettin' hot in here, so take off all your clothes," I encourage you to ignore him, especially if you're outside.

I say this because, with the warm weather, I've begun to see body parts that should only be exposed during medical examinations or lavatory visits. And I'm afraid it's only going to get worse.

For that reason, I've set up a color-coded nudity alert system designed to defend Americans against the gruesome sights that are sure to come with spring and summer.

As a public service, I'm sharing it with you.

Code yellow

This low-priority alert will be in effect whenever the temperature hits 60 degrees.

You would think you'd be safe from near nudity when it's only 28 degrees above freezing. But the truth is, you're not. Because the people who come outside half-naked don't care about temperature. To them, it's always gettin' hot in here. And therefore, any time is a good time to take off their clothes.

The sights Americans are most likely to see during code yellow include the following:

Low-cut blouses revealing breasts etched with squiggly lines reminiscent of rivers on relief maps.

Jeans and midriff shirts that cut off circulation. This look, which features hip fat pushed up past the top of the jeans and hanging just beneath the bottom of the shirt, is always accompanied by a back tattoo.

And finally, the skirt, split almost to the neck, showcasing the varicose-vein convention taking place at the back of the knee.

When code yellow is in place, Americans are advised to wear dark sunglasses and a pasted-on grin, and avoid eating roast pork after 9 p.m.

None of this will keep you from seeing body parts. But you're pretty much guaranteed not to have nightmares about them.

Code orange

This medium-priority alert goes into effect when the temperature hits 75 degrees.

At this temperature, everyone you don't want to see naked will begin to think that they, too, look good in low-rise jeans.

That's why, during code orange, there is always the potential for a crack epidemic.

No, not that kind of crack. The kind of crack we see when people with boulder butts wear low-rise jeans. The kind of crack we see when men insist on mowing the lawn in last summer's shorts. Which reminds me, guys. If you haven't at least done a few push-ups--we're not even talking weights here--please do not wear a wife beater. You have breasts. Somebody may just beat you.

This brings us to the torso concern that is most prevalent during code orange. The concern lies primarily with women (because most men's guts are fat, not wrinkly) and deals with the stomach area.

Ladies, when code orange is in effect, if your stomach looks like chitlins, curdled milk or an old baseball glove, please fasten the last three buttons on your shirt. Do not, I repeat, do not, wear a navel ring.

To the rest of you, when code orange is in place, you are advised to wear oversized black knit hats.

If you encounter crack, chitlins or curdled milk, pull the hat down to your chin. Then duck and cover until you receive the all-clear signal.

Code red

This high-priority alert goes into effect when the temperature hits 80 degrees.

At this temperature, you will see people with multiple jawlines and gargantuan breasts parading downtown with only strings covering their implants.

You will see Daisy Dukes. But Daisy won't be wearing them. Mabel will. And her thighs will resemble day-old oatmeal.

You will see brazen attempts to publicly display body parts that should be seen only by mothers, spouses or doctors. These attempts will be camouflaged by Poom-Poom pants, string bikinis or thongs.

During code red, Americans will need to carry duct tape and plastic at all times.

If, during this heightened state of alert, you encounter string-bedecked implants, oatmeal thighs or any medically unidentifiable body part, follow these instructions carefully.

Pull the plastic over your head. Wrap the duct tape around it. And wait.

You won't have to see that stuff much longer.

America The Bootyful

Sure our way of life is triflin'. But is there any place better?

Lately I've been hearing the phrase, "We've got to protect the American way of life." Which seems strange, because neither I nor the people uttering that phrase really know what that way of life is. How could we?

We live in a society where kids are on Ritalin, parents are on Prozac and reality is a show where people eat worms. The only ones keeping it real are Pookie and Laqueesha. But their reality is a far cry from that of Buffy and Bif.

So if you want me to pin down exactly what constitutes the American way of life, you'll excuse me for having a hard time doing so. Because the reality is, there are so many Americans living so many different ways of life that it's sort of like a bag of *Lay's*. Nobody can pick just one.

Now I know that some of you are looking at this and preparing to deliver a Bill of Rights-quoting, Constitution-thumping "That's what makes America great" diatribe. And that's cool. But I've found that flag-wavers like you are often the same people trying to deny your neighbors access to whatever they believe to be the American dream.

Besides, I think it's best that we skip the speeches and get to the real issue. What is the American way of life, and why should we protect it?

In these uncertain times, when there's so much is at stake, I feel obligated to at least try to provide answers.

What is our way of life, you ask?

In my estimation, it's the God-given right to be triflin'.

If you're too busy to make your kid a peanut butter and

jelly sandwich, you can buy Johnny a prepackaged monstrosity, pop it in the microwave, and run to your meeting. That's triflin'. But that's the American way.

If you're a stay-at-home mom, you, too, can be triflin'. Sort of like a minivan commercial. Picture it: An overwhelmed soccer mom drives her five kids to karate, marching band, swim class, basketball and transcendental meditation. After dropping off the last one, she takes off her housecoat, pulls off her scarf and turns into J. Lo. Then a handsome guy pops out of the cup holder. The voiceover: "Buy the Solomon Transporter, and take your kids to so much crap you'll never have to see them again. Taxes, tags and title extra."

Okay, maybe that's a little extreme. But our way of life is extremely triflin'. Especially on television.

Got dimples in your booty? Get plastic surgery on *The Swan*. Don't have a husband? Get *Married by America*. And if your instant marriage doesn't work out, don't worry your pretty little head about it. Because in our way of life, we provide instant therapy.

Can't get along with your hubby? We'll get Dr. Phil to call you stupid on the air. Need a kinder, gentler approach to your problem? Oprah's got a new guy to call you screwed up. Want something a little more hardcore? Take your philandering husband on Jerry Springer, where you and his Russian midget lover can rip him a new one.

Perhaps your problem isn't a relationship. Maybe you're just unemployed. No problem. If you're buff, you can be a contestant on *Survivor*, where you can rummage for food in remote, exotic locales with no real possibility of starving. And as an added bonus, you can lie, cheat and steal from fellow jobless people, thus transplanting the American way of life to the farthest corners of the world.

Sure, it's triflin'. But hey, that's the American way.

Where else but America can a woman wear fake hair, fake eyes, fake eyelashes, fake eyebrows, fake nails, fake breasts, fake buttocks, and have the audacity to say she wants a real man?

For that matter, where else can a real man wear all those things and try to convince other real men that he's a real woman?

Only in America do you have the right to ignore the gigantic death warning on cigarettes, buy them anyway, then go back and sue the people who sold them to you.

Do you think there's another country where you can walk into McDonald's, pay them to feed you Big Macs, french fries, Shamrock shakes and baked apple pies, then sue them for making you fat?

Is there someplace else where you can drink yourself into a permanent stupor, then apply for disability when your liver goes?

Of course not. You know why? Because nobody else is that triflin'.

But even with all our foibles, even with all our problems, even with all our quirks, I say God bless America. There's not a better place on the planet.

That's why we've got to protect our way of life. Even if it is triflin'.

Keepin' It Wheel

Sure our weather's bad. But our drivers are worse

Manhattan has cabbies who think an inch is sufficient space to cut you off on Broadway--at 200 miles an hour. Detroit's expressways have potholes so perilous they make *The Matrix Reloaded* chase scenes look like a game of dodgeball. But there are few places more dangerous to drive than Philadelphia.

Granted, our drivers don't morph into gun-toting agents with superpowers. But our bad drivers are real, and if you don't look out, they'll get you.

As it gets warmer, your chances of being victimized by bad drivers will increase. And because I need you to survive long enough to read my next book, I feel compelled to tell you how to avoid them.

Before I proceed, I have to warn you: Some of what I'm about to say may offend.

But hey, I'm just keeping it wheel.

Guys blasting hip-hop

Some people might see this as sour grapes, because for years I secretly wanted to be a guy whose car could blast hip-hop. So in the interest of full disclosure, I'll share my car history.

The cars I've owned have always been equipped with factory sound systems, and therefore incapable of blasting anything louder than static. In fact, my last car--a 1989 Nissan with a flat paint job, varicose veins, door rust and tea-saucer sized speakers--was so pitiful that it was outrun by a ParaTransit van on the expressway.

Now that you know I'm hatin', I can speak frankly.

Guys who blast hip-hop are dangerous behind the wheel because their profanity-laced music makes them overly aggressive. Studies have shown that they are 5,000 times more likely to shoot you in a fit of road rage than, say, really mean old ladies in supermarket parking lots.

Not only that, their style of dress renders these guys incapable of driving safely. When your pants are slung low about your thighs, and your boots are heavier than cement blocks, it's impossible to move your foot quickly from one pedal to the other. Which means you can't brake.

Loud music plus aggressiveness plus immovable feet equals accidents.

Women with excessive makeup, weaves or tans

Again, in the interest of full disclosure, I'll admit that I once dated a girl who wore a whole lot of makeup and sported an excessive weave. Still paying for that mistake--literally.

But anyway, now that you know I'm hatin', I can speak frankly.

Girls with really big weaves and lots of makeup are most dangerous during morning rush hour, when they're running late for work, and on weekends, when they're trying to beat the 10 o'clock deadline for free admittance to the club.

At these crucial times, these made-up and beweaved women will try to drive with their knees while simultaneously applying makeup, combing hair and smearing on suntan lotion.

This is not to say these chicks don't use their cars' safety features. Fact is, they're the drivers most likely to use mirrors. Just not to look at the traffic around them.

These women believe every mirror, including the ones in their cars, are there for the sole purpose of checking their appearance.

Mirrors plus weaves plus makeup plus suntans

equal accidents.

People with Jesus license plates

I am a Christian. I believe in the Lord. I pray, read my Bible and attend a church where I am active in ministry. But I've got to keep it real. People with "You've Got a Friend in Jesus" license plates are dangerous.

Perhaps--and I'm just speculating here--this is because they don't drive as often as other people. Maybe they're used to driving only once or twice a week--to church and to the market. Or maybe they drive erratically because they're trying to prove that they're insured by a higher authority.

Okay. I don't know what makes them dangerous. But the facts don't lie.

Jesus license plates are most often displayed by people with big hats and Cadillacs. And when your car's that long, you can't wear a big hat, 'cause you can't see, which means you have to slow down, which means you disrupt the flow of traffic for hours on end.

Nothing against the license plates. But if Jesus is really your friend, let it show in the way you live, not the way you drive.

In the meantime, readers, let's be careful out there. The streets is watchin'.

The Submissive Supervisor

And other workplace horror stories.

Everybody has workplace horror stories. That boss with wax-covered, wirelike hair growing, forest-like, out of his ears. That co-worker who smells like he's washed up with a hoagie. The supervisor whose breath is eerily reminiscent of hot, steamy garbage.

But there's more to workplace horror than the look and smell of it. There's also the sheer terror of dealing with people who bring their household habits to the job.

Women who arrive in heels and change into old, dirty slippers, for instance. Or men who believe they must wear the same funky drawers for weeks in order for their favorite team's winning streak to continue.

If you, like me, have worked in an office and seen people lose it under the stress of delivering a service, manufacturing a product or smelling their stinky co-workers, you know exactly what I mean.

But for those who've never had the pleasure of working with the industrially insane, I'd like to share with you two of the best workplace horrors I've ever heard about.

Company monikers, job titles and individual names have been deleted or changed to protect the guilty.

Freak Nasty, Esquire

Once upon a time, in a galaxy called downtown Philadelphia, there was a law firm that I'm now convinced was the prototype for the madcap sitcom *Ally McBeal*. This firm consisted of many characters, including, but not limited to: the relative who came in and slept on the floor, the secretary whose pants were stapled together and the young clerk who spent countless hours shooting rubber bands at his co-workers.

But there was no character who endured like Freak Nasty, esquire.

You see, Freak Nasty had a habit of convincing young women that they resembled a martial arts instructor he once knew. Once the women were under Freak Nasty's spell, he'd get them to reenact a scene from some long-ago karate class.

The scene? Freak Nasty on the floor, with a high heel in the back of his neck, and the woman sitting over him in a chair.

While his unwitting dominatrix had him down, the flush-faced Freak Nasty would turn his head and stare up at the woman's ... um, worldly goods.

When it came out that nearly every woman in the firm--fat, skinny, short, tall, black, white and Asian--looked like his old martial arts instructor, Freak Nasty's secret was out.

In the real world that type of thing might result in a lawsuit. In the original *Ally McBeal* miniseries, it got him a promotion.

Criminals R Us

My cousin was home on break from college, and she needed a job--fast. She didn't have time to go through the traditional interview process that a real job would require, so she went with the job that promised to put her to work the day after she filled out the application.

Of course this was a place where a light lunch was a 40 and a blunt, and stress relief was an after-work rumble, complete with legions of teenaged boobs running and jumping over cars.

For the sake of anonymity, let's call the place *Criminals R Us*.

On the first day of my cousin's orientation, when new employees were being trained to deliver their telemarketing lines correctly, the trainer asked a few key questions. Among them was this one:

"How many people will have to leave to go see their probation officers?"

Half the people in the room raised their hands. Then things got worse.

One of my cousin's male co-workers took a liking to her. And during a break, when he managed to get her alone, he laid his rap down.

"Yeah baby, you know I just came home." He left off the vital phrase, "from jail."

After my cousin got him to explain what he meant by "came home," she asked him what he'd done.

"I shot this dude."

"Ummmm. Oh."

Gee, you think if she dated him, he'd do her the honor of shooting her, too?

More, More, More

I once crashed a truck into a plane while working at the airport. Another time, I watched two co-workers ride a little red wagon up and down the hallowed halls of *Philadelphia Weekly*.

But the way I figure it, you don't need to hear every workplace horror story to know what you have to do.

If it's football season and your co-worker is wearing the same underwear repeatedly, ask to move to another cubicle. If the secretary smells like she's carrying day-old halibut in her purse, update your resume.

And if Freak Nasty ever becomes your boss, get out your spike heels. You just might get a promotion.

Foot loose

Expose no toes before it's time ... It's never time for nasty ones.

My 2-year-old daughter, Eve, loves beauty products.

Sometimes she knocks LaVeta's eye shadow off the dresser and smears it all over her cheeks. Other times she smuggles lipstick from LaVeta's purse and draws Bozo the Clown-like lines around her lips.

But it wasn't till last week, when Eve demanded nail polish so she could paint her toenails, that I knew she'd made an early transition from toddler to little girl. You see, the nail polish thing shows that Eve knows summer is coming and it's time for ladies to start caring for their feet.

I'm not trying to be sexist here. But men don't wear open-toed sandals too often. Nor do we frequently wear shoes that expose our heels. Women, on the other hand, wear a lot of both--especially when it gets warm.

That means women's feet are usually visible during this time of year. And if you're going to have your feet out like that, you need to keep the public in mind.

There are certain things we just don't need to see. And for the good of all of us, I'll list them now.

Heel Crust

My yearly concern for heel crust began last week, on the first 80-degree day of the year. I was minding my own business, walking back to the office during my lunch break in Center City, when I spied my first glimpse of sandpaper-like heel matter.

The woman looked normal. She was wearing a business skirt and a nice blouse, and she had her hair done up just so. Then she stopped at the light and stood in front of me.

You know how you look around while you're standing on the corner, waiting for the light to change? Well, that's what I did. I looked across the street and saw the McDonald's on the corner. I looked behind me and saw people coming out of the Convention Center. I looked in front of me and saw strands of the woman's hair blowing in the wind.

And then I looked down.

The back of her heel looked like a relief map. The skin had apparently been neglected for quite some time. It was thick, orange and crusty, and there were lightning-shaped cracks extending across the surface.

I wanted to put her in a headlock and yell for a pedicurist. I wanted to take her to the store and buy her a lifetime supply of pumice stones. I wanted to pull out a hammer and chisel, and carve away the layers of dead skin.

I did nothing. And I'm ashamed.

Raggedy Toenails

If you're going to have your toes out, ladies, please familiarize yourself with toenail clippers. They're relatively cheap, and they're available in most drug stores.

Don't be walkin' 'round with your toenails hanging over the edge of your shoes like you're about to go rock climbing with no hands. I know that many of you have men who love you so much (or are so afraid of your deadly toenails) that they won't tell you.

Fortunately, I don't have to live with you. And since I'd hear your toenails dragging on the ground if you ever tried to creep up behind me, you can't surprise me. So I'm free to tell you this, and I will.

Cut your toenails. And after you finish cutting them, smooth them out with an emery board.

You'll make everyone's life easier because we won't have to look at your feet. And maybe, just maybe, you'll stop tearing 3-inch holes in your stockings.

Funky Toes

There were many choices here. Hammer toes. Bunions. Corns. Long toes (which I happen to suffer from). But I decided not to include anything that would require surgical intervention. Therefore, I settled on the funk factor.

There's no excuse for women to have funky feet. If you're wearing shoes that allow air to get between the bottom of your foot and your shoe, there's only one reason for your feet to stink.

You didn't wash them.

Now, I know that women's bodies are different than men's. Most of you don't sweat as profusely as we do, and the chemical makeup of your sweat is different as well. But there are certain areas of the body that have to be washed well and often. Your feet are one such area.

And so, in the interest of making sure you ladies get the message, I offer this short review.

Please don't put on sandals knowing that you're subjecting us to yesterday's funk. Please don't walk around with foot crust, knowing that pedicures are only $20. Please don't keep your toenails raggedy when clippers, emery boards and pumice stones are readily available.

Got it? Good. Walk in peace, my sisters. Just take care of your feet while you do.